All Day Is a Long Time

DAVID SANCHEZ

All Day Is a Long Time

HARPER

An Imprint of HarperCollins*Publishers*

ALL DAY IS A LONG TIME. Copyright © 2022 by David Sanchez. All rights reserved. Printed in the United States of America. No part of this book may be used or reproduced in any manner whatsoever without written permission except in the case of brief quotations embodied in critical articles and reviews. For information, address HarperCollins Publishers, 195 Broadway, New York, NY 10007.

HarperCollins books may be purchased for educational, business, or sales promotional use. For information, please email the Special Markets Department at SPsales@harpercollins.com.

FIRST EDITION

Designed by Chloe Foster

Library of Congress Cataloging-in-Publication Data has been applied for.
ISBN 978-0-358-57201-5

Printed in the United States of America
1 2021
4500843857

*For my parents, whose unconditional love
has contextualized my entire life*

All Day Is a Long Time

Prologue

HERE IS THE TRICK: compartmentalize your life. Rationalization becomes much easier that way. You've got one thing over here, and another over there. People who have affairs, or at least people who are good at having affairs, are masters of this. A shrink told me about this one time like it was a diagnosis. But I thought it was a pretty decent trick.

Don't think about your childhood. Put your anger in one box and your depression in another. Those two things will be hard to look at together.

If you are going to take a woman's purse on the street, don't think about how she looks like one of your friends' moms. Someone who picked you up from school or made you peanut butter sandwiches and lemonade on summer days. If you absolutely have to think about this, think about it later. Put her in a box and say she is just some lady spending her husband's holiday bonus checks. Nobody's ever given you a holiday bonus.

You might be expecting a big cathartic breakdown. Where everything you have ever done will catch up to you, and you will cry and beg for repentance. You will gnash your teeth and rend your garments. The light of God will break into your heart and free you from the bondage of self; you will turn your life around. This might never happen. If it happens, then you have failed at compartmentalization.

You might call someone from your past, an ex-girlfriend, say, and the conversation might be much quicker than you imagined. Where you expected a reckoning, sympathy, you might find someone anxious to get off the phone. You might realize that your actions have hurt people. You might realize that she really, really doesn't care. Your self-pity may come to an end. You might cry for hours into a bare mattress in an empty room in a halfway house. You might drench the bed until it sponges up, and you might crack a window and soak the filters of your cigarettes until you can't breathe through them. This is not compartmentalization. Put her in a box. Call her names. Stop crying for god's sake.

Being broke is unavoidable. Come-ups are, unfortunately, largely case by case. Remember: nobody likes their job.

Go for food stamps. Wait in line all day at the office downtown in those hard plastic chairs; lie about your work and living situation. Ignore the electric whir from the fluorescent lights and try not to sweat too much. It's a long wait 'cause they hate parting with their money. Then it's another few weeks to get the EBT card in the mail.

Some corner stores will let you buy beer or cigarettes with EBT. These stores are found in bad neighborhoods and are unaffiliated with national chains. Some drug dealers will take EBT fifty cents on the dollar.

You can look for drywall in dumpsters and cut it into little rocks, bag it up, and sell it to crackheads. But if the cops find it, they will charge you with *possession with intent to distribute* as if it was real crack. That was Nancy Reagan's doing. And you'll have a bunch of pissed-off crackheads looking for you.

It wasn't until later that I learned the game I was playing is called "Hey, Mister."

Everybody has done it at some point. You're too young to buy booze. You take your money and just kinda loiter around outside a liquor store. You don't want to be too near the entrance because the guy behind the counter might see you, and sometimes those guys can get on their cowboy shit and come yelling at you or call the police. You wait for someone to walk up, you give them a look, and then you say, "Hey, Mister." Probably not those exact words. But you ask them to buy you a bottle. You give them your money. And depending on what type of person they are, they just might do it.

Some guys just want to help out. It's what keeps the rich tradition alive. They see you and your friend huddled up, nervous and stammering, fighting over which one will have to go ask, dropping your voice a few octaves to seem older, holding out a few crumpled bills, and they think about some summer night when they were a kid, when they played "Hey, Mister" themselves and showed up to a friend's house or a lake party with a bottle of vodka and everyone cheered. When they had a drunk, sloppy kiss with the cute girl from geometry class and threw up in the pool.

Then there are the drunks. Not the homeless and wet-brained drunks, but the ones just barely clinging to their earthly possessions. They pull up in the parking lot in a beat-to-shit Honda or an old F-150 that makes a sound like dogs barking as it drives. They step out in a bathrobe or slippers or whatever stained clothes combination they have specially chosen for shuffling around their house, sleep-watching cable. These guys won't give you the time of the day. They're myopic; they'll walk right past you and ignore your little voice clearing, the crack in your pubescent throat as you say "Hey, Mister."

Then there's the homeless ones, the guys who smell like sour sweat and dried shit, that have beards and sinewy, skinny bodies like stray dogs—harsh tans and open sores, cuts on their knuckles, burn marks and faded stick-and-poke tattoos on their knotty forearms. No teeth and three shirts. They will want you to pay them for their services, or at least buy them a little something. These are the guys that when you see them take their first pull of the day, you feel it. Like when you stop at a gas station after a day of landscaping in August, when you open the cooler and take the first pop off a Gatorade before you even make it up to the register. That's how they pull. You feel the world relax, you feel the tightness all around you just up and unfold, even though you didn't even know it was there before, and you weren't even the one taking the drink.

It's rare to witness someone achieve satisfaction so quickly and so fully.

Anyways, the third kind, that's the kind of Mister I said "Hey, Mister" to after I slipped away from home and hopped the Greyhound from Tampa to Key West, in the middle of a ninety-degree night, fourteen years old, still shivering from the long bus ride when he walked up.

When you smoke crack or inject coke, you can't hear for about thirty seconds. All you get is a sound like a 747 landing down the street, or an aluminum train howling past your face. It sounds like water on fire. Like a ghost fight or a panther crying. Some people call this "getting your bell rung." Medically, I think it is some sort of cocaine-induced tinnitus.

The structure of a cocaine molecule looks like a boat. Hanging off the bow is a single nitrogen, or base, called an amine, which makes the molecule slightly basic. In the powdered form, this nitrogen is bonded to a hydrogen ion to make a hydrochloride salt. If you take that salt and mix it with a slightly stronger base such as baking soda or ammonia in water, then the hydrochloride ion gets broken off and bonds to the stronger base; if you heat this mixture, then the hydrochloride gets burned away. Without the hydrogen ion, the amine, or base, becomes free. You see where this is going.

Heat a pot with water, don't let it boil; turn the knob to five or six. Mix three parts coke and one part baking soda in a Pyrex, drizzle water on it so it gets soggy. Put the Pyrex in the heated water. Keep it on the stove and stir a little bit. Let it bubble until it turns to mashed potatoes, then it will congeal into a pancake. Pop it off the burner and put it under cold water. Once cooled, take out the pancake and carve it up into little rocks. The kitchen will smell like burnt rubber for a few hours.

Talk to it while it cooks. That will make the whole process go easier, faster; I don't know why — that's psychology, or maybe magic.

It's called crack because the baking soda makes a little cracking sound when it's getting burned. It's the sound of carbon dioxide being released from the molecule as it changes states, same as Rice Krispies.

Everyone knows that meth fucks up your teeth, but it isn't the meth, actually, that rots them out. It's not candy. The meth just makes you stop producing saliva. Spit helps kill germs and bacteria in the mouth, so without it your gums and your teeth fester. The bacteria grows and grows and crawls in the soft tissue down around your roots, all in the holes you nervously chew in your cheeks until your teeth start turning yellow, brown, black, and disappearing. Spit is disgusting, but, like many things, the alternative is worse.

When you shoot cheap meth, your mouth fills up with oil, typically Coleman camper fuel. Most meth is bad meth, and all you need to make bad meth is some Sudafed, lithium ion batteries, Coleman camper fuel, Drano, table salt, and a two-liter bottle. It's kind of a pain because you have to shake the bottle and twist the cap every few seconds. Getting the lithium strips out of the batteries isn't easy, either; you have to pierce the casing and pry off the top, then remove the insides and unroll them. During the reaction, the oil works as the solvent so it doesn't break down, and it slides right up your veins and drips into your mouth. You will smell it, too, but it isn't in the air. It tastes like how you'd expect. Like gasoline and slippery, bitter cum.

Find the bars where young white people drink in a neighborhood that was Black two years ago. "Up-and-coming" areas. Somewhere with a lot of foot traffic and wait around when it starts to die out. The people here want to get robbed, I swear — it adds to the "experience." They'll give it away. Look for boat shoes, polos, expensive purses, look for baby blue and yellow. Look for drunk people; they are less predictable but also less likely to call the cops.

If you don't have a gun, use a knife. If you don't have a knife, use a needle and say you're sick. You can do this by an ATM, but there are usually cameras there, so hang back a little.

Why do you do it?

Common answers: You are running from something. Trauma, especially. You were raised wrong, you didn't know any better. It's genetic and one or both of your parents are the same way. You are incapable of living life on life's terms. You don't care about other people. You have exceptionally weak willpower. You are too sensitive. You are a delicate, misunderstood genius like those musicians who die choking on their own vomit or the writers who put a shotgun in their mouth. The ugliness of the world is too much for you. You have a disease.

These are all flimsy excuses.

The lizard brain, the reptilian brain, the amygdala: these refer to the same thing. A little almond-shaped bunch of nerves in your brain responsible for decision-making and emotional responses. They are a part of the limbic system, which is at the head of the mesolimbic pathway. The pleasure pathway. The reward system. It's the oldest part of the brain; it's been around since mammals evolved from reptiles, since we had scales instead of hair and walked around on four legs licking each other with forked tongues.

A little clump of neurons in the center bottom of the brain projects the dopamine out through other areas of the brain, and when it hits the end of the trail, you feel a positive sensation, a reward, and you become satisfied. But the pathway is unable to distinguish drugs from food or sex because it is all translated into one language, dopamine. Where a good meal will release about 50 units of dopamine and sex releases 200, a tiny shot of crystal meth releases more than 1,000. Once the ventral tegmental area (VTA) takes on this much dopamine, the whole system gets hijacked. Over time, the system can become accustomed to these unnatural amounts of dopamine, and satisfaction and reward sensations become harder to achieve. This is why the need for drugs takes over the need for food or other basic necessities. Once the pleasure pathway is rewired, you'll spend all your time obsessing about what rewired it, about how to get it.

This has its own flimsiness, too. Just more blame shifting. It'll probably get "disproved" in five years, anyways.

"What are you doing down here? You on vacation with your parents or something?" he asked me.

Back then, everyone who was older than twenty seemed just old to me. But looking back, he couldn't have been older than thirty-five. He was small with the look of hard living. His stick-and-poke tattoo was of a five-leaf clover and had a date underneath it. I gave him ten bucks and told him I wanted the most of the cheapest. He got a fifth of Popov and told me that it was $9.99. He said he covered the tax with his own.

"You're gonna need some money. How much money you got on you?" he asked.

I told him the truth. And the truth was that after my bus ticket, which I got round-trip, I had $215 saved up from painting houses all summer.

He told me I was lucky I found him because there were folks down here who would rob me or worse. But he said he isn't from Florida, so he doesn't behave like that. He just comes down for the winter when it gets too cold in Chicago.

I said, "I'm here to see a girl." And it was the truth, too. That was my plan, as far as it went. Nicole. She was a grade up from me and down here on vacation with her parents and her sisters, and she told me that as long as her parents don't find out, I could come down, her sisters would be cool about it. And she told me that she had been thinking about me since school ended and that she can't get me out of her head and her dreams, and she said I'm crazy for doing this, but she didn't want to stop me.

He whistled low and passed me the bottle. He asked me where she was staying and steered me down a residential street — pink and yellow A-frame bungalows with fences, little shotgun houses with four-step porches and two windows to the right of every door. We walked through the streets quick, and he told me he had to make a stop.

"How old are you?" he asked.

"Sixteen," I lied.

"You ever done coke before?"

"Yeah, a few times," I lied again.

We turned north up the island, to where there's a trailer park tucked between some scrub palmettos and a few ugly trees. Just about a dozen single-wides propped up on cinder blocks and broken skirting. Sitting a couple hundred yards in between the airport and the high-tide mark, where the washed-up horseshoe crabs dry out, and the sand fleas burrow blindly and chew on the wet, gray shore.

If you can afford it, get your hands on a multivitamin. Meth leeches your body of vitamin D_3, which is how you absorb calcium. Without calcium, your hair starts to fall out; it just up and leaves without warning, and everything else gets fragile: your nails, your skin. You'll get a cut opening a water bottle.

Eat at least a Snickers bar every day, steal an orange from the gas station on Sundays. Snickers has everything you need. Calcium, minerals, protein. It's not the highest calorie-to-cost ratio, but it's up there. The best ratio is the plastic-wrapped danishes: the Big Texas and the Jumbo Honey Bun. They typically run for $1.50 to $2, and they are 560 calories. Figuring at $1.75, that's 320 calories per dollar. A cheeseburger from

McDonald's is about 300. A can of Coke is 140, and a small bag of Lay's is 160.

Crack and meth cause excess concentrations of norepinephrine in your brain. Meth makes your brain produce more of it, but crack inhibits your brain's ability to reabsorb it. The crack binds to the protein that is supposed to get rid of the norepinephrine, so it gets stranded, like its car got stolen, and it builds up in your extra-cellular space and kicks neurotransmission into high gear.

The norepinephrine looks and acts just like adrenaline. It initiates fight-or-flight, but it really gets you in the brain. It enhances your focus and your attention, your retrieval of memories. It makes you vigilant. It allows you to process sensory information fast and effectively; you see the delicate patterns of the world and react to them, you organize them, you set up a system and derive meaning from it, courses of action. You become hyperaware to enhance your chances of survival. But if you aren't in danger, if you're just sitting around shooting coke, and there is no reason to fight or flee, then you might start to pick up the spare bits of yourself and the world, to organize it into a made-up pattern that is better left unseen — a frightening structure of delusion and paranoia, full of filled-in gaps and illogical connections, a golem of mad information. You have to feed this instinct, too, your brain's loud craving. You have to give it books.

Good books for junkies: Read Dante, read *Moby Dick* while you're high, get lost in the chapters that luxuriate on the different kinds of rope and how to tie knots. Read *Notes from the Underground,* Ellison's *Invisible Man* if you are withdrawing. *The Waves* or Faulkner if you haven't slept in a few days. Mostly, don't go north of 1950. Stay away from the beatniks — they don't know what the fuck they're talking about. And memoirs are whiny. Especially don't read those books about rock stars; it'll just piss you off because of how broke you are. *Trainspotting* is pretty good, but heroin is for suicidal teens. If you've got enough meth to last you a while, give *Paradise Lost* a run. See if that does anything for you.

A book is just time-released information. Just ink on paper. A word, one datum in a relatively simple system of information transmission. But there are moments, moments where the information piles up and time stops and everything becomes greater than the sum of its parts. The rhythm of the words and their shades of meaning match up for one brief second. It's the passage of time that allows this to happen. Beginning and end give the duration a special fertile quality. Search for these moments when you read. If you can't find them, toss the book.

I wasn't scared on the bus, and I wasn't scared on the walk. I wasn't scared of this rotten-toothed third type of man, either, and I brought a knife with me in my backpack, and I was young and fast, the fastest kid on any team I'd ever been on, at least one of the fastest. But next to the moonlit, sun-bleached sign that said POINCIANA MOBILE in baby blue letters on pale pink wood, I saw an urgency in his eyes that I'd never seen anywhere before. I don't know what you would call it: an emptiness, a wildness, a heat.

It stunned me for a second when he said, "Give me fifty bucks."

"What for?"

"You wanna get right before you see this girl, right?"

I handed him the money and followed him into the rows of trailers. He pointed to a spot outside one of them, handed me the bottle, and told me to wait there. He disappeared up the short steps and through a door that someone opened for him.

I started to get a little scared, but mostly just that my money was gone. I knew a few kids who did coke, and I had seen it before, and I wanted to try it, so excitement started to take the place of the fear in my gut, and besides why wouldn't he just take all of my money if he was gonna rob me?

I still remember the address. I peeped at the numbers as I was walking in: 1641. Inside it was all peely wallpaper and fast-food garbage. Rising damp soaking upward from the wet ground, making those cheap particleboard walls turn to patches of mushy, wet fiber. He was sitting on the couch with some woman. She was big, and she was wearing a bathing suit with a wifebeater over it. She was bigger than me and him put together; she had light freckles up and down her fleshy arms, dyed hair that was the color of red velvet cake, a rhinestone stud in her tiny nose, a tattoo of a dragonfly on her neck, an indistinguishable one on her upper back. She had more, but they were hidden when I first walked in. She smiled at me as soon as she saw me; she had pretty dimples and crooked small teeth. All her features were small, but her face was enormous.

She was the biggest person I had ever seen.

They parted for me to sit down between them, and I did. I had my backpack on my lap. She lifted it off of me and put it under the table.

He was holding a stem, and he took some rock from off a piece of Saran Wrap on the table, loaded it, and passed it to me. I didn't know what it was or what to do with it, but I held it like I did. Mister was holding a lighter, and I put the stem to my mouth.

He said, "Slow. Inhale slowly."

And I did.

First, the ringing.

The 747.

The aluminum train.

The sound of water on fire.

Sitting there, in between Mister and the Giantess, I lived the whole rest of my life — decades of misery and haste, ecstasy and boredom; only to be born again, live exactly fourteen more years, and find myself unchanged back on that couch, in between Mister and the Giantess. I spent all my money and it reappeared and I spent it again. With his hand on my crotch, and her untied bathing suit hanging down like rotten fruit over her stomach, she kneads her gigantic, freckled bosom; she grabs my wrist and places my open palm against her chest, my other hand still holding the stem. She smiles and shows me her pretty dimples, and he starts unzipping my pants, putting his mouth closer to me.

Through my wide teenage eyes on the milky canvas of her breasts, I see myself, older, uglier, dirtier, stroking my dick on a white couch. I taste the oil of every cheap meth shot I'll ever do. I hear the ghost fight and the crack of broken fingers, and I feel that Gatorade gulp. I see a thousand stoves with bubbling Pyrex measuring cups and cold, clear spoons on the floor of gas station bathrooms. Shotguns and AR-15s, steaks and mean dogs, my shaking hand pointing a needle at a pair of boat shoes. I see bookcases falling over and lizards in the prehistoric jungle eating Snickers bars, unrolling lithium batteries with their claws.

I see the boat of a cocaine molecule sailing across her chest, bobbing and losing its hydrogen ion — the base becoming free.

In my pants, I feel him and the crackling of crossed wires, the overstimulation — the compartments of my life, memories and hard-earned knowledge, exploding and flooding into one another, flowing out to the silent, dark waters of the Gulf.

1

EVERYTHING HAPPENED FAST FOR YEARS. A couple months on the street, a couple months in jail, a couple in the psych or the halfway and back on the street again. This job, that job, always only for a couple months or weeks before something happened. Sober for a few months and then not. A couple months on this pill or that one — Effexor, Risperdal, Lamictal, Seroquel, Latuda, Lexapro, Trazodone. I couldn't even tell you what I was taking when I was taking it. I would wake up in the halfway house before a bellboy shift and think I had to go trim hedges. I would wake up in the psych thinking I was in the park, ready to go hit a lick. I would bang a speedball, come to my senses, and think it was time for Richard Simmons. I would wake up in jail nervous that I missed my PO appointment. Everything was time soup in my head. Dumplings of memories and noodley thoughts.

I woke up in a crack motel at three in the afternoon thinking it was three in the morning; I looked for my keys for thirty minutes, thinking I had to go to the warehouse by the airport to bag newspapers and run my route, only to remember that I didn't have a car and my newspaper job didn't start for another three years.

Even the books I read would twist and braid into one another. I would start a new chapter of whatever Hemingway and in that half of a blank page get mixed up, get confused, and brace myself for eighty pages of Milton, expecting verse, expecting marching feet, poetic contractions and confusion, and, instead, see those little sprints of sentences — simplicity and Paris, Africa, Cuba, Spain, godless expatriation, modernity, and all the hunting and the fishing and the bullfighting and the love not love, Key West, the only place of his I knew — and then I would forget again, and ready myself for a fight with Milton, with God and tangled meaning, no underlying iceberg truths, but God on the surface snarled in an iambic jungle, and then my roommate would come into our tiny halfway house apartment and bitch about his ex-wife, or the chow carts would get rolled in, or the public library was closing for the night, or the compulsions would come up through my stomach and force me out into the world.

In the story of my life that replays constantly in some faraway lobe in my brain, narration begins and ends and starts over. It gets longer every time, more details are added, and they change — they get brighter or dimmer and sometimes are just wholly fabricated. It replays in jumbled scenes, in that "unused" percentage of the brain. It sucks up the moments as soon as they are passed and incorporates them in its own logic. The story I tell myself constantly, about who I am and what I have done, where I am headed. And from that story, a memory is not what it seems, a dead recollection from a static cabinet in the brain — it is an echo from the unending narration in the other room, and the narrator is a creation of the main character, not the other way around. If you listen, if you unlock a door to a quiet room and put your ear to the wall, you can hear him running his mouth.

My brother used to say he could remember everything. That most people's first memories start when they are around four or five but that he could remember much earlier than that. Six months, one year. He said he could remember the day I was born, as if it had just happened. On that day, he was three, and he came to the hospital with my sister and brother, who had been watching him while my mom was in labor. And when he went there to meet me for the first time, he brought his favorite toys with him. No one told him to do this; they just said he was going to meet his brother, and he got an idea. He brought two little plastic dinosaurs, a T. rex and a ptero-dactyl. When he would play with them at home, he would hold his forefinger and his thumb to his temple, and he would pinch and then drag his pinched fingers to the toy, to draw his consciousness, his immaterial self — the thoughts, the emo-tions, the fears, and secret joys — into the toy, so the T. rex could be him, could enjoy his child's mind, and he could en-joy its powerful body, and he could run freely.

And when he saw me in my mother's arms, wrapped up

and staring silently at the bright room and the faces crowding around me, he patted me on the head, and he put his fingers to my soft baby head and dragged my newborn consciousness into the pterodactyl, and then he did it at his own temple and dragged himself into the T. rex.

My mom asked him, "What are you doing?"

He told her and she laughed, and she asked him if he loves his brother, and he said he does. And he said that since he is older and bigger, he is the T. rex, and I am the pterodactyl. And she laughed and my older siblings laughed, and he went and sat down on the little couch in the hospital room and played with the toys, put me in his right hand and flew me around while the T. rex stayed on the ground and marched and roared.

I wonder what he dragged from my head then, at that youngest age, getting older by the second. What did I come here with? Did I recognize myself as something individual, as something separate from the blaring hospital light, the arms of my mother, the beeping machines, the nurses running in and out and down the hall?

In that most vital of moments, that moment in which I was supposed to first conceive of myself as discrete, to orient myself within the three dimensions of life on Earth, to understand my physical extension into the world of things, my limitations as a shape of organic matter bound by the laws of physics and geometry, in that moment I was ripped from my mewling, helpless self, and I was given the wings of a gigantic prehistoric bird. And there, with that first blast of the light and noise of the world, where I was supposed to learn laws, rules, codes of conduct, the base-grounding relation on which all other conceptions and relations are built — I am my body and my body is me — I was given flight instead, and the rest of my life after that was one giant lamentation, one quick screeching fall and yearning for the sky. Your first moments on Earth should be a humbling experience, but I was given power. Without that foundational understanding, there was only disappointment and restlessness. Endless desire pulling at my worldly chains.

And this was the only thing I could think of as a possible reason for why I behaved the way that I did, why I felt the way that I felt, which was the animating question of all the therapies and theories of addiction. All those possible reasons that never held water for me because they weren't specific or real. Because maybe my brother forgot to put my consciousness back in my head, and I was never wedded to my body in the way that I should have been.

In a letter he wrote me while I was in jail, my brother reminded me of how I used to cry when I watched the sun go down. He wrote me from college. College, just the sound of it conjured images of a different world, a better world, girls and boys and books and parties, big fuck-all parties that went late, where everyone got drunk, but no one ended up in jail or sucking crack smoke from a plastic tube, squirting meth into their arms for days that turn into weeks that turn into months. No, these parties took place at night, and then they ended, and everyone went to class the next day or maybe slept in and texted each other about what a good time they had.

I wondered what he thought about me. I wondered if he told girls that his little brother was off the map, in jail or in the wind, a junkie with an engine in his ass that won't let him be happy. I wondered whether he turned this into a sob story to get attention and sympathy from the pretty girls in scarves and $1,500 winter coats. Or whether he didn't tell anyone anything about me, just kept it close to the chest and pretended or just plain forgot. I would think about him whenever things would slow down, or, I guess, just imagine his life. I would sit on my bunk and wonder what he was up to, wonder how pretty the girls were, how expensive the coats were, how good the books were.

I was surprised when I got the letter. I wasn't expecting anything. It had been a few years. But I was doubly surprised at how sentimental it was. I mean, it tore me up to read. And we have the same exact handwriting, so in a way it was like a letter I had written to myself.

He said he thinks about me a lot. He said he thinks about when we were kids, when Mom and Dad were off work, and the whole family would go to the beach, and we would bodysurf or throw the football and sit around and eat sandwiches from a cooler and get sun-kissed and tired and wait for the day to come to its gentle, pretty close. On those beach days where it seemed like our family was in a commercial or something. We would all stand there on the beach, staring out over the Gulf, watching the sun go low and dim and turn the blue sky pink and turn the water into oiled metal. Our dad would pull us together and tell us to watch for the green flash in the second after the last sliver of sun dipped into the water. The green flash, my brother said, he thinks we saw it once or twice, but he can't remember if he just started saying he saw it and manufactured a memory for it or if, really and truly, we watched for it and it came. Our dad would try to explain to us what the flash was — a trick of the light that you could only see at certain latitudes, certain atmospheres, and clear conditions. He would try to explain the science of it all as best he could.

But what my brother wrote that really tore me up was something that I had forgotten. He said, one summer when I was probably around five or so, every time we would stand there and watch the sun set, as it started to get low, I would cry. Cry these adult tears, he wrote, quiet and solemn. Not wailing or throwing a fit but grown-up tears, like the sunset was a funeral. When anyone asked me what was wrong, I would say that I didn't want the sun to go away, how did we know it would come back, and that I wasn't ready. And when someone would ask, *Ready for what?* I would struggle to think of what to say, and I would just blurt out that I didn't know, but I wasn't ready, I didn't want it, and I would ask my mom to make it stop, please, to make it stay there, and she would explain that it was gonna come back. This happens every day, she would say, this is natural and it's pretty and it's all part of a cycle. But my brother could see that it was still there, that grief.

So, on one of the evenings, he tried to help me. He put his arm around my skinny shoulders, and he waved goodbye to the sun, and he said, "Thank you, see you tomorrow," and so I held out my hand and copied him, and I waved, and I said my proper goodbye, tears drying on my cheeks, and I was surprised at how it made me feel better. He somehow knew that that would help, the formal acknowledgment.

I'm sitting on my bunk reading this letter, and it's ripping me up. I mean, it's loosening up all this shit in my chest, and it's turning into hot liquid and moving up into my face and sinuses and my eyes. And I get up, still holding the letter, and I go to the bathroom to be alone and maybe try to cry a little, but the whole unit is a goddamn panopticon, and the toilets have these little two-foot walls next to them. When I sit on them everyone, the COs and everyone else, can see, and so I just sit there on the toilet and fight the rising heat in my chest, and I beat it back, and I move my mind from thinking about the sun and its setting, and I fold up the letter and put it in the back of my bunk drawer.

I never laughed.

In the waning months of my junior year, the last few months of school I would ever attend, I was coming out of a three-day Xanax blackout, and I was in art class drawing an elephant. After days of talking cursive, slurring, and repeating myself, I was starting to be able to remember stuff if I concentrated really hard. Our teacher gave us an assignment to draw something, anything in the room. We had those big 18-by-24-inch sketch pads that open from the top.

I was sitting there, and I was wondering what day of the week it was, wondering what things had happened in the past few days that I would need to be brought up to speed on.

I was trying to build my consciousness back up brick by brick, remembering who I was and what the rules of my life were, one by one. Just the facts. *You are alive. Alive is the opposite of dead. Alive is something and dead is nothing. You became alive, snatched out of the dead nothing, in October. In 1991. This is your name. This is your address. You are sixteen years old. You live in Tampa, Florida, America, a city in a state in a country on planet Earth, a big island in an unimaginable sea. You have a family, a family is the people that you live with, the people who created you and your brothers and sisters. You are the youngest and you have two brothers and two sisters. You have black hair and hazel eyes. You like old movies. It is March. You go to school. This is school. This is where kids go during the day.*

And while I am piecing this stuff together, I am staring at this clay figurine of an elephant and drawing it on the sketch pad. I am drawing it in blue pencil, and I am trying to copy it as best I can. To make it look perfect, exactly as I see it on the table. I am concentrating as hard as I have ever concentrated. My tongue is sticking out of the corner of my mouth, and I am chewing on it lightly like a small piece of chicken. *You are in art class. Art is different from the other classes, math and science and history. Art is just basically colors and copying. You've gotta copy this elephant, so you can leave class. Art class is in the morning. The morning is when the sun . . .*

And on and on, as I keep drawing. And after I finish the elephant, I am proud of it. It looks almost exactly like the elephant on the table, and so I add a few spirals on its fat body.

Small, few, tasteful. Simple three-ring spirals, like a shell. And I rub my eyes and stand up, and I am shocked to see that the elephant is no more than four inches tall, in the southeast corner of the giant, yawning sketch pad. I thought I had drawn it large and in the center. I sat back down and got really close to it. I couldn't believe how small it was, and the straight lines I thought I was making were actually kind of fuzzy, hard to see, minute little shakes from my unsteady hand.

My art teacher looked over my shoulder and made a small gasp, and she told me to sign it, so I did.

And she ripped it from the sketch pad, got everyone's attention, and said, "Do you see what he did?

"Do you see?

"The tiny elephant alone in the corner of the big white page? Alone in the big wide world? This is how you use white space. This is how you use the page to create emotion."

She tacked my drawing up to the board in front of all the drawings from the actual art kids who practiced and hung out in that cluttered room in their free time, and who I occasionally sold acid or pills to in the parking lot.

At lunch, I took my girlfriend into the room and showed her my drawing. It looked so funny up there, just basically a blank page blocking a few intricate still-lifes.

I said, "She thinks I did it on purpose. But really I was just fucked up. I thought I was drawing it regular sized!"

I sat on the table, and I started laughing and pointing at the way my page took up so much space, covering the shading and the meticulous care of the advanced art kids' drawings, and I lost control laughing until my sides hurt. But my girl-friend wasn't laughing. She was standing there really close to the board, staring at the elephant, and looking back at me with a kind of disappointment and faraway sadness that I was just starting to get used to.

"It's really good," she said, "she's right. It does look lonely."

I was still laughing, harder now.

There was another time, later, in county, when all of us were gathered around the TV in the dayroom watching *Cops*, but I couldn't be sure if I actually laughed that time.

I was sitting in Palm Beach County Jail on Gun Club Road, in the middle of the narrow hallways of the twelve-story maze in the main detention center. And I wasn't fed up with it yet, so I was watching TV and playing spades or whatever, that's why I think I might have laughed. The novelty was still there.

Cops was on and we watched an episode that took place outside of Vegas. Everyone was making fun of the fat-necked cops and the tweakers and hookers with ice in their socks and tits falling out of their shirts. Everyone was having a good time watching it—the trailer parks way out from the strip, the cops and their self-serious monologues to the camera.

But then another episode came on, and after that song and the stylized opening montage, this real Bubba of a cop is driv-ing his squad car and talking about what he does to unwind after work, talking about golf, and how necessary it is to de-compress, and how he and some other deputies go out and play on their days off, about how many great golf courses are around.

And all the while he is talking, underneath his fat head there is a little strip of text that says "Palm Beach County, FL." Everyone goes apeshit. We immediately start trying to recognize the stuff he is driving by, all the palm trees in the dark purple night, shut-down strip malls and abandoned houses. The text on the screen says he is in Lake Worth now.

I figure there must have been at least five guys in my unit who were from Lake Worth, and they start yelling "L-Dub" and "Gunshine." The cops pull into one of these flat, low projects, a few square blocks of fenced-in Section 8 apartments, and I recognize it as one of the only spots north of Lauderdale and south of Tampa that you can get heroin that isn't cut to shit. I had been walking down that street just a few months ago, and I suspect some of the guys in my pod even more recently. The cops creep through the fenced-in projects in that squad car with the camera whirring; people on the street staring or trying not to stare as the cops drive slow and swivel their heads around, looking for someone to beat up or shake down. They pull up to one of the units and this dreaded guy is leaning on his car; he is on the phone and wearing a big red-striped polo. He looks up and sees the car, and he drops his phone and bolts.

"Oh shit. I know that boy," someone in the dayroom screamed, "that's Russ."

Russ is cutting through yards, turning corners, ducking under clotheslines, and dumping shit out of his pockets. The

cameraman is shaking and struggling, and the cops are yelling after him and chasing. We are all screaming now and the
whole unit is on their feet, crowded around the TV.

"Go, Russ, go."

"Shake his ass."

"Jump the fence."

And for a second, we were all excited, watching Russ go
rabbit-fast, turning corners, and putting moves on these red-
neck cops. We were invested in the idea of Russ getting away.
We forgot that we were watching TV, and we knew how this
was gonna end, that Russ and the cop had been cast for these
roles long, long ago, and the ending had been written long
before the cop spied Russ's red polo and his dreads. There's
a whole gang of cops now, and they are working on cutting
Russ off, on bottlenecking him.

He jumps up onto the chain-link fence, and one cop grabs
his hair and puts him down hard. He sits on Russ's back and
twists his arms and cuffs him and takes out his wallet, looks
at his ID and then the camera, and says, "Russell Jackson, you
are under arrest."

"Ayyy, I told you that was him," the kid in the dayroom said.

The cop takes Russ to the car and lays him down on the
hood. They've swarmed up now, naturally. There are three
or four squad cars, and all these cops are excited to be on TV,
bustling around, talking shit. One of the cops throws a Ziploc
with a few bundles of heroin down next to him on the hood.

"He's got priors, man. He's fucked. He's got warrants," the
kid in the dayroom says.

And just as he says that, one of the cops comes out of the car and says to the camera, "This isn't the perp's first rodeo. He was busted for selling H two years ago, warrants on VOP, failure to appear."

The cop turns to Russ. "What do you think the judge will think of this, Russell?"

He doesn't say anything. He just stares at the flashing lights with his cheek laying on the cold hood of the squad car and that "I'm fucked" look in his eyes.

The cop grabs him by the cuffs and says, "Russell Jackson, you're goin' to Gun Club." And everyone in the unit falls over themselves laughing, grabbing each other's blues and slapping one another on the arm, half expecting this buzz-cut cop to walk Russ into our unit right at that moment, just step out from the TV and plop him down on the bench to sit in the dayroom with everyone else.

But I can't be sure if I laughed along with them. I can imagine it both ways. I can see myself laughing wild with my hands at the absurdity of it all, the TV like a mirror and Russ with that dumb look on his face, the play-by-play from his buddy and the fucked-up chronology of it all, the idea that Russ was probably sitting in some other unit in the same jail right now. I can see myself stomping my feet laughing, reaching out and putting my hand on the guy next to me, slapping his chest or arm, feeling the vibrations of him laughing too.

Or I can imagine myself sitting there, alone in the back while the crowd erupts in front of me, stone-faced, not even cracking a smile, thinking about how maybe Russ was shipped up the road already or maybe he was five years into his sentence and about to get out. Maybe he had already gotten out. Maybe he was leaning on the hood of his car, talking into his phone in a big red-striped polo right now, living in some fucked-up time loop like daytime *Cops* reruns.

I'm gonna say I laughed. Laughed along with everyone else. And so, it hadn't been years because that just couldn't be right. That couldn't be possible. No one goes that long without laughing.

2

I WAS PICKING BOOKS off the shelves, trying them out and putting them away. My mom was working nights, but she had Tuesdays off, and on those days, she would take me to the library after school. I had turned eight a few months before, and she was letting me roam around for as long as I wanted. We went to pick up a book she had reserved at the front desk, and then she just sat there while I looked around. She wasn't hurrying me, but she wasn't reading her book, either. She was just at the table, looking at me or at the unopened laminated cover. Reading was the thing we shared. There were days when we would spend all morning reading together on the couch in silence. Around that time, I found out that I could read big fat books—three, four, five hundred pages—and this made everyone proud because they were designed for young adults, and I was just a kid. My teachers, my mom, they all thought it was remarkable, a sign that I was smart. But really, I think it was just a sign that I was bored, that I would do anything to relieve that restlessness in my heart. I could sit for hours if something had my attention. I could lose whole days to preoccupation, and I actively sought it out. But as I got older, my mom used to say, *School isn't designed for people like you.* And I think I knew what she meant. It was the crowd and the noise and the authority, the direction, the rapid changing of subjects. But most of all the person at the front of the room, trying to corral my attention, tell me what to do, what to focus on.

The organized silence of the library after school was different. It was freedom even with its rigid system of order. The order made it freer somehow. I memorized the Dewey decimal system first, like a map, so I could move through the place with ease. It was a one-story, one-room library with a checkout desk in the middle and shelves radiating out from there. Around that time, I wanted to be a "nature photographer," that was my answer whenever someone asked me what I wanted to be when I grew up. My teachers always got a kick out of this. They would laugh and wonder to themselves, *Where did he get that idea, a nature photographer, what does that even mean?* So I went to the Natural Science section, 500–599, and I walked around, looking at the books I couldn't fully understand, looking for pictures within them. I went to the magazines on the far right wall to find *National Geographic* and look for a picture that called out to me. I could look at a single picture for as long as I could read. They didn't seem so different to me.

There was a jaguar in the jungle, under the thick, lush can-opy, stepping over a log — his face a pool of sad determination, a look resting on the bones of his skull, a look of unmistak-able loneliness and despair. His eyes, deep set into the wall of singular bone that made his head, cast onto the ground. He looked suicidal, like he wanted to be anywhere else but inside of his spots, like he wanted to be the ground that he walked over, the trees that quivered in the wind, the insect, the frog. He wanted to be the steamy, tepid air.

I looked at him for a long time. Then I looked at the trees and everything else, all that he wanted to be, all that he couldn't see that he already was. I memorized him. I mem-orized the picture as a flat single object, a splattering of col-ored inks. I stuck the picture into the condensed flame in my head until it was red and glowing. I seared it onto my mind, and it never left.

My mom sat down beside me to see what I was looking at. These, I think, were her favorite times; this, her favorite part about me. A sign that maybe — despite my intense bursts of anger or sadness, despite my growing secrecy, my withdrawal from the world, or the fights or trouble at school — I would be okay somehow. These afternoons we shared grew into a mu-tual understanding between us, until I got older and meaner, more restless, less patient, less open to subtle things, and she would scream at me in the middle of the night, stuff like *I don't even know who you are anymore!* when I'd steal some-thing from the house or money out of her purse and disap-pear for days or get arrested or end up in the hospital. She put her pointer finger right between the jaguar's ears and moved it back and forth a few times as if to give him the pet that he wanted so badly.

She said, "We have to go. You can check this out if you want."

But I put it back where I found it, the image already branded onto my memory. I could look at it whenever I wanted.

She put her hand on the back of my neck and rubbed it, kissed my forehead.

That night I barely slept. I lay in my bed and closed my eyes and just went there, to the jungle, for hours on end; my brother dead asleep next to me in his bed. I was concentrating so hard, I thought it might wake him up.

The next day at school, we were filling out a worksheet to put in a time capsule. It was the very end of 1999, and we were about to leave for winter break. I was supposed to open the time capsule when I was eighteen, on New Year's in 2010. The worksheet was titled "Who I Am in 1999," and the questions were prompted.

My name is _____.

My favorite food is _____.

My favorite hobbies are _____.

When I grow up I want to be _____.

And at the very end there was a question: I wonder why _____. So that we could look back and see what made our little brains whir in 1999. What did we wonder? Maybe the question was to show us how much we learned over the ten years, how we now knew the answer to that which we used to wonder about, or maybe the question was there to show us how little we, where it really mattered, changed. Our favorite foods and hobbies were all different, they'd matured or phased out, but at the beginning and the end, our names and our secret little questions were still the same.

I wrote, *I wonder why God chose me to be a part of mankind.*

And I put my paper into the box and sealed it up, and I never opened it again. I lost it somewhere along the way, thrown out in some move or another before the assigned date. In 2010, eighteen years old, I had no hobbies, and I didn't eat very much, but there were things that were unchanged, I think.

Over the break, my dad and I went to the Everglades, just me and him. On Christmas, he got me a pocketknife in a little cardboard box, and he said he would take me camping, just the two of us, which he knew was something I always wanted to do. He had made me the same promise the year before, but we never made the trip. I was obsessed with "nature." My family waited for it to pass like a regular childhood phase, for me to move on to cars or planes or Star Wars, but it never did. So that was who I was. If you wanted to interact with me, "nature" was the way to do it, the medium to get into my head. My dad knew. He recognized a kindred spirit, a twinned brain. Or maybe this is made-up, and no one knew that I really liked nature, and my dad just happened to take me camping one winter when he wasn't working, and maybe no one thought about it like that, "nature" vs. whatever else there was. Maybe that was just some weird thing in my head, and I projected it out onto everyone else, and people actually didn't think or wonder about what was going on in my head half as much as I thought they did.

It was early January, and it was just me and him in Big Cypress. We ate freeze-dried food, and we sweated and traipsed through the wetlands, through the marshes and the rivers of grass. It was so quiet out there, that's what I remember most — the long-legged herons moving silently through the marsh, their steps high and slight; the still water not lapping against anything, sitting solid like black glass; alligators motionless in the grass by the water, their mouths stuck open, getting fed off the sun's heat like a flower — so much life, so little noise. Even my dad and I didn't talk. On the drive down we stopped at a roadside bar, and I got a hamburger, and we sat there eating and drinking in silence. We drove to the park with the radio off, the wheels gliding over the highway with a dull roll until we got to the dirt roads where they crunched and jumped, and then came to a stop, and we pitched our tent without saying anything.

I was sitting, stripping the bark off a stick with my new knife, exposing the clean, soft white wood underneath. My dad was starting a fire, and I stood up and went and gathered up some wood and placed it down by the pit, and we sat there in mutual understanding as the world got dark, and we stared at the fast, silent flames licking the night. I took out my knife and the stick, and I picked up where I left off, stripping the bark and contemplating the meat of it, wondering what I could try to carve. He pulled the cooler out of the trunk, and we sat there until we got tired and unrolled our sleeping bags and put out the fire and went to bed. In the night, I realized, not in any particular terms but wordlessly in my gut, just how pointless talking is. How it might be our most vain invention. Existing only to rend ourselves from the world, to call out and express our perceived particularities and burdens, to push them out and pass them on to other people. Narcissistic and useless. Vain in both senses. A symptom of our most basic predicament, the dead-ended frustration of being animal plus something. Every word a plea to make it stop.

He woke me up in the dawn with a light push, and I stepped outside, and it was cold, or at least cold for me, and we ate some oatmeal, and he pulled out a map and we both stared at it for a while, committing it to memory, before we started walking through the trees. In the morning sun, the lizards and the snakes and even the birds woke up but didn't make noise. The banana spiders sat fat and silent, glowing on their dewy webs in the sun.

We found our trail, and we walked for a few miles through the cleared brush, and suddenly my dad put his hand back and stopped me where I was walking. I was looking over at the knees of the cypress trees to our right, and when his hand touched me, I looked forward up the trail. There was a panther in the middle of the clearing eating a baby boar. He was facing us as he ate, and when he heard us, he looked up, and I saw his eyes sunken into his singular bone, cast down in horrible sadness. He was shorter than I expected, no more than two feet tall, and he had a GPS collar tight and heavy around his neck. His shoulders were hunched, and his mouth was wet; his eyes were wild and empty; his fat tail was raised above his head — he looked like the very demon of grief, of thwarted desire. He looked into our eyes and screamed, loud and shrill, the first words I had heard in a day. Birds flew out of the trees. He screamed again, this time longer, and it contained within it the whole alphabet of human struggle, the wailing of babies, the banging of gavels, gunshots and ignitions, tears and howls, music and racket, television static and microphone feedback, the whole clamor of existence and, under all of it, the ur-emotion from which all other emotions are born — pain, confused and terrified pain.

As he loped off, he broke our spell, and we started talking again. The ospreys started calling in the air, and the trees started to rustle in the wind. The whole world got loud, and I asked my dad all the questions I could think of, and he told me how endangered the Florida panther is, how it's the only big cat this side of the Mississippi, how they used to roam all the way up to Tampa and farther, how there are only about a hundred of them left.

"What was on his neck?" I asked.

"A GPS collar, so they can know where he is."

"Why do they need to know where he is?"

"Just to gather information, to learn more about his habits," he said, "so they can help."

When we got back to the camp, we made another fire, and he passed out on the lawn chair he brought. I sat there staring at my fleshy white stick, wondering what to try to carve. I wished there was a way to carve sound, to carve out the panther's scream and have it physical and in my pocket. And while I thought about that, I stuck the knife's point into the wood and I turned it, over and over, twirled it in my hands until it dug a perfectly symmetrical hole right in the middle of the stick, just a little black void that I couldn't see the bottom of in the weak firelight.

By the time I was sixteen, the family unit had whittled down to three. Everyone gone from the house but me, the youngest. My older siblings had a few kids apiece and were living in different corners of the city, and my brother was away at school. So it was just me and my parents, and in the moments when all three of us were home, the house was full of tension and anger — my dad by the TV, my mom in her bed, me in my room. My grades were slipping; I was checked out of school, ditching all the time. Waking up in the morning, they were usually already gone, and I'd send an email from their computer. I would pick and choose my days wisely or else just go to school for a little and then leave. Until I stopped even caring about that.

My tolerance was starting to rise. I was itchy and barely holding on to consciousness, trying to catch it as it fell away from me. It was a Wednesday or maybe Tuesday in the afternoon, and I had been on a couch all day in some hot house with a couple of people I barely knew, dropouts and older kids. The light in there was yellow, and the wallpaper was yellow too. We were doing blues and nodding out on the sweaty couch. It was one of those sticky days that seemed to go on for a week, just didn't end and got so empty that I felt like I was going crazy. Whenever I did oxys, I would get angry, frustrated. I think it was the way they slowed up my brain and made it hard to think, the world was harsh and confusing when I couldn't think quick. I'd get mad and try to make it slow down a little, try to just get everyone and everything to not bother me while I could figure out what was going on. And for some reason, this stayed right there with all the good feelings. The side effects would fight it out in my blood or on the ridges and valleys of my brain, and the good feeling, the physical goodness of my body, would still be there, I'd still feel opiate good, light in my chest and heavy in my limbs and face, but mentally, the frustration was there too. The dissonance was strange. It was like whenever someone would talk, I would get mad at them for interrupting my feeling good.

And it was around eleven that morning when the pale little guy whose couch it was started fixing shots. He had long, thin hair and scrawny joints. His lips were always blue, and his eyes always pinned, lost out to the opiates, and he was next to me on the couch, bent forward over the crowded coffee table — bottle cap overturned, needle cap off, spoon laid flat. We were getting blues three for twenty dollars back then, the government not yet caught on to the doctors, and, like I said, the day was long and scratchy.

After she got out of school, my girlfriend came and picked me up. We went up to the top story of a parking garage downtown and sat on the hood of her car and watched the sun go down. We sat there for about two hours; she did most of the talking. We lay there and put our backs against the windshield. She rested her head on my chest, and the sky was fat and purple and dark. She wanted to have sex, I could tell, but the way she kept trying to hold my hand was pissing me off. The way she touched my shoulder or kissed my neck, everything was frustrating me, and I wanted her to just shut up and stay still and let me sit there on the hood of the car. And she looked at me and asked, "What have you even been doing all day?"

I figured she probably thought I was just sitting around, smoking weed and maybe drinking beers with some fuck-ups. When we first started dating, I wasn't as bad off. I didn't need to get real fucked up because she made me feel so good — sneaking around and having sex wherever we could, in the back seat of her car or in some side room at a party, in the bathrooms at school or in her bed after her parents would go to sleep. We couldn't keep our hands off each other. I was caught up in feeling all the shit I never felt before, young love, just enjoying someone, wanting to be around them, wanting to talk and kiss and hold hands and feel the soft otherness of her body. It felt good enough to keep me from hard drugs for a while, just drinking and smoking weed, maybe taking a pill or two at a party, so maybe she thought I wasn't as bad off as I was.

We would talk on the phone for hours until our phones ran out of battery, and we had to go sit by an outlet to talk some more. I just couldn't believe that I actually felt this way. I couldn't wait to go to school so I could see her. I couldn't wait to kiss her the second we were alone. And I would lay my head in her lap and she would touch my face, and I would let her, and she would tell me that I was pretty, had pretty eyes, that she liked the way my eyelashes were long and dark, or that I was smart, or funny, that she liked it when I smiled, and I believed her for some reason, the whole thing just felt secretive and new. I didn't know people were allowed to be this way with each other, to say these things to each other. The first time I saw her room, I knew I was in something different; being in a girl's room was like being in a garden or a coral reef, so much color and life, pink and blue and green, and it was big, and her bed was soft and full-sized. There were pictures all over the walls of her and her friends and nice soft clothes strewn around. There were cute things everywhere; it was like Candy Land. Standing in the middle of that room, I felt like I was behind the scenes somewhere I wasn't supposed to be, somewhere people like me weren't allowed. She had a closet I could walk into, and I would; I would walk in there and sit down in the middle of all the colorful fabrics and listen to the quiet, the air crowded with all of her pretty things. I started to say nice things to her too, to touch her face, and kiss her nice and soft, and say that I liked her eyes, their particular shock of blue, and I liked the way her cheeks hit her jaw, and the way the sunlight looked on her hair, or how she made me laugh, or how we talked on the phone forever.

And all of that must have been sitting in my head somewhere while we were on the hood of her car watching the lights of the night below us and the wind ruffling the bay, but I couldn't find it. She tried to hold my hand again, and I shook it off, and she said, "What is with you?"

"I don't know," I said. "I'm tired."

"From what?"

The high from the blues had been dissipating and the irritability was sticking around, getting stronger. "I don't know. Bullshit," I said.

And she looked at me, with skepticism and sadness, and said again, "What have you been doing all day?"

I was annoyed. I knew that her friends had told her about me from the beginning, that even before we were together, she had heard things at school about what a fuckup I was, that I was mean and high and crazy. It pissed me off that she didn't believe them, that she wouldn't see what was clear to everyone else. She knew I took that bus to Key West years ago but never made it to her hotel. What did she think I was doing? I thought she should know by now, deep down. I had two bars and two blues in my pocket, and the kid from earlier had given me a rig, and I just wanted to go home, to be left alone so I could feel good without any distractions.

"I told you. I'm just tired." My voice was low and scratchy and slow from the opiates.

"Well, maybe you should go home, then," she said, and she had a few tears on her cheeks now, shining slippery in that pink parking lot light.

"Yeah."

So I started walking over to the staircase to leave, and she said, "I can drive you."

"I want to walk."

It was about ten, and if I meandered by the bay, it would take me an hour or so to walk home. I wanted to give it time, so my mom would be asleep when I got back. She didn't want me to stay out so late, but I was young, and I had endless energy to fight about this kind of stuff. She was old and tired from work and worry, and she would run out of steam when we fought. She had to pick her battles carefully. I had texted her earlier, telling her I was studying with my girlfriend, and I doubt she believed I was studying, but she liked my girlfriend, so she probably just convinced herself that I was with her being sweet and normal like a teenager. I chewed up the Xanax as soon as I got in the stairs of the parking garage, and I sucked on the bitterness as I walked home.

I unlocked the door quiet and took off my shoes, slid past my dad on the couch, and went to the kitchen to get a cup of water and a spoon. I made sure to be extra quiet while I walked past my mom's open door, but I was already slurring my movements. I had been spending a lot of time reading the internet drug forums. They taught me stuff I couldn't have ever come up with on my own. I studied them harder than I'd ever studied for school. I thought about Xanax as a central nervous system depressant, slowing down my neurotransmission. I thought about it in magical terms, as a GABA receptor agonist. GABA, an amino acid that controls a few little ion channels in the brain, the benzo locking on to the receptor and opening the channels, allowing chloride into the cell, which makes it resistant to depolarization, which quiets down the neurons and stops some of the electric firing and basically makes you an idiot, slows your thoughts and your feelings, makes you dumb and happy, but it also slows your heart rate and your breathing way down. The forums said don't mix it with opiates because they do the same.

I put the spoon and water and lighter in the bathroom, and

I went to my room to get my brother's old laptop. I wrapped it in a towel and turned on the shower and tried to jack off a little bit. I laid the towel out on the floor of the bathroom and sat on it while I looked for porn on the tiny little screen, trying to find whatever it was I wanted to watch. Drugs and sex had fused into two sides of the same thing. Whenever I was high, I wanted to jack off or have sex, not sweet back-seat-of-the-car sex like my girlfriend wanted to have, but something else, something uglier, and whenever I did that, I wanted to be high. I always tried to time it up as best as I could so that right when I was feeling as high as possible, I could come, and it would push me just a little bit higher. I could feel the Xanax in my blood, but the oxys from the afternoon basically felt all gone by now, so I wasn't worried about doing too much. I fixed my shot. I crushed both of the pills up as fine as I could with a quarter. I poured the powder into the spoon. I had cheap headphones on, and I was just listening to the sounds of porn while I worked, but I was completely focused. I dripped the water into the spoon and my hands were shaking from excitement, the bathroom filling with steam. I tried to guess how long I had been in there, only a few minutes. I didn't want my mom to wake up or get suspicious from hearing the shower for too long.

I thought about the exchange, needle and blood, how it was the perfect way to get high. Smoking, snorting, eating, it was all too delayed, too secondary. This was medical efficiency. Shoot it right where it needs to be, let it run up through the arm, through the veins that twist and turn all through the inside of your body and lead to your heart like the highways downtown, all intersecting and clustering in the same spot, and from there, everywhere else, the brain.

As soon as I slammed it, I fell out — soared for a half a second before my breathing and my heart slowed until they were closer to death than life. The blood left my face and my lips turned blue, and I went to the other place, the silent black swamp of an oxygen-starved brain.

My mom was never asleep. She was sitting awake in her bed in the dark like always, tormented by worry, by nightmares of me doing exactly what I was doing. She found me and the hospitals started, the behavior camps, drug testing, and after-school IOP programs, the tears, and the fights. Whatever tension was in that house flexed even tenser.

3

ENERGY, RAGE, AND TERRIBLE LONGING — still six-
teen, still trying to push these things out of myself, trying to
thrust them onto other people. And so, at a behavior modification facility, I got in trouble for fighting. I don't remember
with who or for what reason, but I was young and angry, and
I itched for a fight everywhere I went. Skinny and stronger
than I looked, I fought with my bones, sharp and protruding,
used them like knives and clubs and unforgiving restraints.
But someone big could throw me clear across a room if they
got a good hold of me. I knew this, and I tried to stay aware
of it.

So, having exhausted most of their punishments, they sent
me to a shrink who would have me sit on the floor and finger-
paint while she played classical music. I couldn't believe it.
Where did they get these ideas? How could this ever become

an actual practice for an actual doctor to do? How did no one in the process of inventing this therapy have even a brief moment of reflection where they thought, *This is fucking ridiculous*?

On the first day, I just rubbed a bunch of colors around on the paper, bored and wanting to show it. But I discovered that I liked the way the paint felt on my hands and the way my wet hands felt on the paper. And then, looking at it, to my surprise, I discovered that I kind of liked the way the colors looked smudged together. I mean, it was nothing to be proud of; it was childlike, but I found it soothing the way the colors were somehow affected by my hands. A texture or a hue, I couldn't decide.

My therapist was, and there was no avoiding this, hot. She was so hot that the other guys would say that maybe they should start more fights so that they could spend time with her painting on the floor. She was young, and she dressed nice in a way that I couldn't understand. She wore vibrant colors and silk blouses; sheer or opaque, they transfixed me. They sucked my eyes in, and I couldn't tell if I was staring at her boobs or at her blouse, and then I would become aware again and try to look away. I sensed that she knew what I was doing, that she was aware of my confusion, and I started to wonder if maybe she was wearing these blouses like Rorschach tests to uncover some kind of pattern in my head.

So much of her life, I thought, must be devoted to color. I couldn't imagine what that would be like. Blouse shopping and choosing, making people paint and then analyzing their paintings, choosing which ones to hang in her office, which ones would match the color scheme of the room. I couldn't imagine a second of her day where she wasn't thinking, in some way or another, about colors. I imagined it was like a language to her. Some kind of secret code through which the world and the people in it revealed their mysterious truths. And I was acutely aware of how simple I must have seemed to someone who could trade within that language. Her, at her desk, living a life of infinite richness, and me, on the floor painting with my hands, without even tools for refinement, like a child. And sometimes I started to resent her for that, for putting me on the floor, for giving me no tools. But other times, I trusted her that it was for the best.

And one day, I walked into her office mad, frustrated at the futility of this exercise, bored at the inactivity of institutionalization. Feeling, like before, that any perceived slight, any small thing that I didn't like, would start another fight. I wanted to fly off the handle; I wanted to leave and just shoot some coke into my neck and let my eyes and ears die violent deaths in my skull. I wanted to shed my body and rise out, but as soon as I walked into the office, I felt all of this fade back into me somewhere. She was wearing a green blouse — light mint green with a natural pattern like stalks of wheat or small horseshoes, and it had a few gold buttons on the front and one halfway up each sleeve, a light green which was not the color of her eyes, or anyone's, but rather brought out some recessed, furtive color that, once hit, revealed itself hiding within the muted, more natural green of her eyes and made them shine like a cat's in the night. She wore a gold necklace that hung close to her throat and had a pattern of two small white pearls on an oval with parallel, flattened sides spaced out every two inches. And the necklace called over to her buttons and then to her watch, which also had a pearl face set onto gold, and all of this was adorning her skin, which was olive but freckled, and her hair, splayed across her shoulders, was brown and contrasted against the light green of the blouse. She stood up when I walked in and drew her curtains to shut out the sun so the light from her desk lamp glowed only on her, and the whole scene struck me as being two-dimensional, like a painting in and of itself, flat but colorful and alive.

"Come in," she said, and I took my place on the ground, which she had already set up for me — the bottles of paint and a plastic box with compartments for storing and mixing them and a small blank canvas not much bigger than a sheet of paper. The classical music was playing lightly, muffled, as if it was coming from under the floor. She asked me how I was doing, and we talked for a few minutes, and then she told me to begin.

The first few sessions, I never knew how to start. I would wait and wait for an idea or something to strike me, but by this time I had gotten better. I had started to be able to just let myself go and see what came out later. The first thing I did was mix some white with the lightest green to lighten it even more. I mixed it around as best I could, and it lightened the green up a little but mostly just marbled it. I took two fingers and swirled them around in the top right corner and made a ball of the marbled green. I mixed red and blue and made two slightly curved, upright lines near the bottom right corner. Using a vibrating motion with my middle finger, I drew a few smaller lines cascading from the tops of each of the curved lines. I stopped and studied the scene. The purple shapes looked like palm trees, so I added small circles in their boughs. Everything was on the right side, and so I drew a thick black vertical line with two fingers bisecting the canvas. Then, I turned it ninety degrees and drew a big black sailboat as accurately as I could resting on the straight line. I turned the canvas back to the way it was and looked up at my therapist; she was answering emails on her computer. I looked at the clock to see how long it had taken. I liked my painting. I thought about asking her if I could keep it. I sat there for a while, and eventually when it became clear that she was really engrossed in what she was doing, I lay down on the ground.

I have a habit where, when I feel overwhelmed, I lie down on the floor. Hardwood is best, but tile is good, too. I lie down and, if I can, I take my shirt off and just try to feel the hard floor underneath me, supporting me. I don't know when or how or why I started it. I think my dad used to do it. I remember seeing him, early in the morning when he didn't think anyone was awake, lying on his back on the floor and just breathing slow and measured, being aware of the air going in and out of him. So, I guess that's where I got it from, but I don't know what made me do it at first. I don't think it was a conscious decision. I think I just saw the floor the way you see a sandwich when you're hungry or a pool when you're hot. And maybe this is some sort of metaphor, some kind of desire for a more abstract kind of stability in my life; only it doesn't feel very figurative. It doesn't feel like a metaphor. It feels like I actually just want to lie on the floor. And maybe all the other stuff — the emotional and social stability — maybe that's the figurative part, the substitute for what I really want, which is to lie on the floor. And so, I had another question without an answer. Or rather, the same question I always have but in another context: Why am I doing this?

She noticed me and looked at the painting, and I told her all this stuff, and she turned the canvas ninety degrees and pointed at the sailboat and said, "Is that you, then? Resting on the hard floor?"

And I shrugged, and I asked, "So, something I was thinking about is, if I always want to lie on the floor and feel stable, but I also do drugs which destabilize stuff, what do I really want? Stability or instability? Or am I just trying to level out or what?"

I thought I was just focused on the wrong thing, like an idiot sitting in a room, feeling too hot and, instead of adjusting the thermostat, turning the volume on the TV up and down.

And she said, "What about this?" motioning to the right side of the canvas.

I said, "Those are palm trees."

She looked at them, nodded, and said, pointing at the green circle in the top corner, "So that makes this the green sun?"

I nodded.

"Why green?" she asked.

I thought for a second, wondering what she would make of my answer, and I said, "Because it's the color of your shirt."

And she looked down at her blouse and raised her eyebrows, but she didn't say anything.

Why green? I asked myself. Because green is good. Green is natural. Green is not white. Angry, empty white. Green is not the murk of black.

"These two different pictures occupying the same canvas indicate your unreconciled relationship with the world outside of yourself."

I was listening.

"The symbolism here is clear. Almost transparent. You are the boat, the oversize boat apart from the sun and the trees. Apart but near. Drawn to the boundary line that separates you. The sun can symbolize divine power and beauty. It is the life-giver; it gives us energy and marks the days and seasons. It is a stabilizer. The fact that it's green emphasizes this even further. Green is the color of energy, of nature and life. The trees are where they belong. They are under the sun, in a row. They may indicate your family. Like a family tree. The family which you are apart from."

She traded in a different language, like I said, the world of colors and symbols. I hadn't noticed, but my hands were still wet with paint, and as I was listening to her, I must have been putting my hands all over the place because I could feel paint on my jaw and chin, could see handprints on my pants and on the carpet in places I don't remember touching.

"So I think it's fitting that you brought up your desire to lie on the hard floor after painting this," she said. "It isn't the floor you want but what's underneath it. The foundation that connects you to everything else. You have a strong compulsion toward beauty, but only as an outsider. You should allow yourself to be a part of it. The line is self-drawn. It's an illusion."

"So is this all painting is? Just a bunch of feelings?" I asked. "Could you do this with, like, a Picasso painting or Van Gogh or something?"

"Yes," she said, as she opened up the cabinet under her desk and got out cleaning supplies. She told me to wash myself off and get some paper towels to clean up my handprints on the floor.

And as I was on my knees scrubbing out the paint, she made a joke. She said, "When I said interact with the world, I didn't mean stain it."

After I got out, a kid I knew from the facility introduced me to Bruce. We drove all the way south to some giant shining building on the water, and we walked into the clean lobby. We avoided eye contact with the doorman and took the elevator to the top floor. Bruce's apartment was all straight lines and marble and gleaming metal appliances. I think he was in real estate or something. We went out to his balcony and smoked a cigarette when we got there. Then we went inside, and Bruce pulled out a fat bag of meth, and we got strung out.

He wore tailored suits and Italian loafers, pink shirts with paisley cuffs turned up by his wrists. He had a strict dental regimen and took handfuls of vitamins and supplements every day to stop the meth from getting to his looks. He had thick blond hair that he kept styled with products. We really hit it off, bonded on some kind of fraternal level, and eventually I started going over there without the other kid. Bruce used to say I was "heroin chic," but really I was just dirty and skinny, wearing clothes with holes, and he knew heroin didn't do it for me. We were speed people. He would give me a couple hundred bucks or an air mattress to sleep on if I jerked off in front of him or his camera. He had some friends who would do the same.

At first, he would just go in the other room, I'd put on some porn, and he'd turn on the video camera, but after a few times, he started hanging out behind me while he did it, hovering and circling like some luxurious buzzard. I'd sit there and feel small, feel how light and wasted away I was. I watched one of the videos once; I looked just like I felt, two inches tall on the TV screen, a pile of bones masturbating in the middle of the open floor plan, natural light all over my body. I couldn't see outside in the video, but I knew that from where I was in the video, I could see boats going by in the bay below. I could see downtown and all the tangential islands, joggers on Bayshore. The sharks and crabs. I watched myself close my eyes and try to concentrate on staying hard, trying to let myself go.

And then after, he would let me read or give me some food, let me take a shower. But he never let me sit on his white couch. He never let me sleep in the guest bed. He had this really big bookshelf that was deep with all kinds of books I'd never heard of. After a while he let me read some of them. He said he had been an English major in college. He said he won a prize for his poetry when he was younger. He asked me if I wanted to hear some of it.

He was a phantom, or maybe I was — we floated in and out of each other's lives without warning. A night or two at his place when outside was too much for me. He bought my piss from me by the bottle, he would put it in an enema, and he said the high was so good it would make you weep.

I told him this was because meth was a salt, it was extremely water-soluble, about half of it comes out untouched in urine. He said he didn't want to hear about that — molecules, solubility.

He said, "Science is the boring man's religion."

I asked him what branch of science he was talking about and he said, "All of it. Jesus Christ, can't anybody understand figurative language?" He was a creature of high drama, and I think he knew that underneath my flat affect, my monotone voice, and quiet clothes, in that running narration in my head, I was too.

He got me to read to him, mostly this poetry anthology by H.D. full of sad, natural images. I would sit at the kitchen table, and he would close his eyes on the couch, or we would go out onto the balcony, and I'd have to read loud over the wind. I started to get pretty into it. It was unlike anything I had ever read, just a running collection of stark pastoral or seaside scenes.

The light passes
from ridge to ridge,
from flower to flower

I asked Bruce, "Why are you always getting me to read this book?"

"I hate H.D.," he said, "but I thought you'd like her."

He said, "Nature is a lie."

The petals reach inward,
The blue tips bend
Toward the bluer heart
And the flowers are lost.

He said, "Not all objects are equal."

I told him that he was wrong. I thought about myself in the video, equal to the air mattress, to the light and the sliding glass doors, to the sleek marble kitchen and the glowing white couch in the background.

shadow seeks shadow,
then both leaf
and leaf-shadow are lost.

"Whatever makes you feel safe, sweetheart," he said.

4

SOMEWHERE ALONG THE WAY in my freshmen year of high school, the wrestling coach found me. Small and wiry and angry, the way I'd been my whole life. I strutted around school like a Thai rooster, not listening to anybody, standing up and walking out of class whenever I felt like it. Not afraid of the upperclassmen like the other freshmen, my brother being one of them. Taking his shit for a decade, I knew that there was nothing behind these kids but a few years and some slick talk. I felt older than them even though I wasn't. I wasn't scared of the teachers or the principals either. I felt older than them, too. These were good qualities for wrestling, and the coach used to brag that he had trained Ray Lewis over in Lakeland when Ray was in high school. He said he was just a skinny kid then. No one knew how good he'd be at football, but my coach saw a wrestler in him, an angry lean kid with a chip on his shoulder who went on to win two state championships. He said Ray's dad was the best wrestler the high school had ever seen, and all Ray cared about was beating his records. So the coach's eye was good, I guess. I was good, too.

The coach taught math, not PE. He taught ninth-grade geometry, and that was how he found me, gone off some pills, sitting in the back of the class with a lip of Grizzly in, spitting into a cup. Wrestling and geometry — the guy was Greek, and he was ugly like an ancient, too, pot-bellied and snub-nosed. And it seems like he could be a role model or something for me, a coach mentor, but he wasn't. We were just two separate weirdos; we didn't have any sort of special relationship. He just taught me how to wrestle and would praise me sometimes in front of the other kids.

In the hot and sweaty room one day after school, he yelled, "Be like him! You know why he's good?"

We were doing King of the Mat, and I was running through the whole team. Starting at the lowest weight classes and moving up, winner advances. I was 112, had been cutting weight all season, so I was second lightest, and I'd already beaten nine of my teammates, and I was working on my tenth, 171. The room was ninety-five degrees, and the mat didn't smell like cleaning chemicals anymore; it was streaked with sweat, stripes of it, puddles of it under our dripping clothes, and, in those puddles, the dirt, the bacteria and the fungi, MRSA and ringworm replicating, staphylococcus looking to move from that desolate, inorganic surface into some open wound, some warm living flesh to infect, some skin to build a red, angry

civilization across, microbes competing for space, and us —
big, fat, and above — competing for space, too.

He said, "He's good because he's mean."

I was bullying my guy, even though he was bigger than me,
and I was feeling mean, digging my chin and my elbows in
wherever I could. I had Saran Wrap around my stomach, and
I was in full sweats, trying to lose weight. I was seeing stars.
I was tired, and when I was trying to move the 189 guy on my
team, I just couldn't do it. He cow-catchered me and slid my
face across the dirty, sweaty mat, and, from there, nose dug
into the rubber foam, I could smell the faint chemical clean-
ers as they dissolved, and he pinned me, and I slunk back to
the wall to rest.

I knew that was only a part of the truth, the mean thing. I
was good because I knew certain things intuitively: angles,
trigonometry, leverage. I understood simple machines. I understood triangles, how they dictated the moves, how the
lines you had to push your opponent on were straight, and
the line you had to take to get to him was straight, and the
line to pin him was straight, too. Three lines connecting and
forming something contained. After cutting weight, after
you strip twenty pounds of round fat off your body, you see
the body is made up of triangles too, stacked on top of each
other and fused together — shoulders to waist, elbow to wrist,
head to chest, hip to knees. Veins growing diagonally across
my arms and chest, down my calf, and intersecting into one
another.

And I understood that wrestling is about hand control.

Your hands, obtuse scalene triangles chopping through the space under your body. The whole match is a fight for the other guy's hands. If you can control them, you draw the angles he travels, and he has no balance and you can do whatever you want. No matter how good you are, if the other guy had your hands, you'd lose. This fact was a sharp and clear reality in tournaments. Burning through early opponents in a tournament, you can tell they don't know this basic secret. You just grab their wrists and take control. But as soon as you get into the later rounds where the competition is stiffer, the fight for the hands gets hard.

One-third hand control, one-third trig, and one-third meanness. Three periods in a match. Wrestling was the Platonic ideal of fighting. I discovered that every fight I ever got into out in the world was a substitute for this, the real thing.

At a tournament in Jacksonville my junior year, my record was twenty and one, but I hadn't wrestled anyone good yet. The year before, I was better, even though my record wasn't. I was locked in then. I was doing the Phoenix House outpatient treatment, and I was passing my drug tests. I had a singleness of purpose. I was swept up in that three-month sweet period, that new relationship period where I was getting everything I wanted. I felt regular, like a regular kid — girlfriend, sports, school, going to parties. All that disappeared in the spring. I started cheating the drug tests, and I got too spread out. And by winter, I was back to being a full-on freak. That is to say, I was back to doing real drugs. I was the two seed going into the two-day tournament. I had been ditching practice, ditching school, ditching my girlfriend. The coke had me light but tired all the time when it wasn't around. We took a van out from school, stayed in some cheap hotel waiting for the big tournament.

At six in the morning, we all filed into the locker room for the weigh-in; a couple hundred boys lining up by weight class and stripping down to step on the scale. All wrestlers have a similar look. I can spot them a mile away, no matter what they actually look like — white, Black, country, city, long hair, short hair, stocky, lanky, doesn't matter — they have a volatile, animal vibe like small predators: stoats or coyotes, piranhas. I'd see them in jail, would recognize them as soon as they walked onto the pod. I'd see them in AA, none of the easiness of baseball or basketball players, the clumsiness of football players. We were like jockeys off our horses, uncomfortable and fast. And these big tournaments were like a tour of the state: one match you'd be wrestling some river rat from Palatka or a rabbit-chaser from a trailer in Clewiston, and then next you'd have some corner kid from North Miami who only knew street noise, was probably scared of cicadas or the rustling of leaves. You'd bump up against some fancy kid from the Palm Beach country clubs who had a summer internship, or the son of a strawberry picker in Ruskin. It was like the army. We all lined up and stripped down and stepped to the scale. The ref pushed his hands onto my nails to see if they were too long, pulled my hair a little, ran his knuckles on my face to make sure I didn't have stubble. Then I stepped on and waited for those little red numbers. I was 112.02 with boxers, and I knew that. I only stepped on the scale to prove it, and then I got off, took my underwear off, and got back on naked. 112.0. I wanted to take time to make sure everyone in my weight class noticed me, that they saw that I knew my body, that I had been cutting. At those weigh-ins, everyone was still tired, scared in their morning nerves. They hadn't come into themselves yet and wouldn't until around nine or ten. They're all jumpy and vulnerable, panicked because of the nudity and the proximity.

I ate a peanut butter and jelly sandwich after I weighed in, drank a blue Gatorade, ate a banana and an apple. After a week of eating nothing, it all tasted flavorful and sweet, even the runty, cheap apple and the unripe banana.

I burned through everyone on the first day, conserved my energy. Two quick, easy first-round pins. I relaxed and waited for the semis the next morning. Just lay out on the bench and watched over the giant gymnasium. Eight mats spread out over the hardwood, sixteen kids wrestling at once, parents yelling from the bleachers, coaches and teammates in the corners. It was a circus of noise and whistles and school colors.

My mom never came to my matches; the whole sport scared her. She hated it. It was too violent, but I rarely lost, so it must not have been me that she was worried about. She didn't want to see me win, see me bully another kid, throw him around, put him on the mat. She didn't want to see what happened when I was in control, when I had someone to ragdoll and choke. My dad, on the other hand, liked to go to these things. It was something about the mass of kids using their bodies, none of the abstract, disembodied word games of socialization that he hated so much. Here we learned more fundamental truths about ourselves and the world, about the mind and body as one instrument, one mechanism. It reminded me of how he was in the summers before I started working, when I was in elementary and middle school, popping up out of nowhere in the middle of June, making me do assignments out of some math workbook he bought at a thrift store. He called it "enrichment." I don't know where he got the idea, but I passed his understanding early, to the point where he couldn't tell if I was solving the problems right or wrong, but he would meticulously check the answers in the back of the book. He would stand there while I jumped through grades, and he would say, *You think the Chinese kids are just screwing around all summer? You think they're afraid of working? You think they're waiting for someone to hand them whatever they want?* I hated it. I hated enrichment like I hated the push-ups and sit-ups he made me do randomly before disappearing back into the vapors of his mind, on the couch or out the front door.

He didn't come to these tournaments far out of town, so he wasn't in Jacksonville, but at the ones in Tampa, he would stand quietly in the corner of the gym and watch me. He was a good baseball player when he was younger, but he didn't know anything about wrestling. That didn't stop him from hypothesizing, picking up terms, and telling me what I needed to work on. He understood angles, and he understood being mean, but he never mentioned anything about hand control.

* * *

Another weigh-in the next morning with a one-pound al-
lowance. In the semis, I had some senior who looked like he
had cut as much weight as I did. He had long hair in a skull
cap and a couple tattoos. He was strong and manic but dumb.
I could tell he wanted to fight me. I thought he was going
to be good, but he wasn't. The first round was just stalking,
hand-fighting, and jerking around. Both of us toe to toe and
locked up ear to ear. I pulled his head down, and he resisted
as hard as he could, so I let go and all his resistance popped
him up, and I shot down and double-leg tripped him. As soon
as he went down, he bounced up, and we were back ear to
ear. I did the same thing again, but when I shot down, I did a
low single leg, grabbed his ankle and pushed with my shoulder into his shin, bent his knee straight and forced him down.
I climbed his body, half-nelson turned him and thought it
was over, but he was strong. He fought me, and I couldn't
pin him, but I could feel him getting tired. He won the coin
toss in the second and deferred. I took top and laced my left
leg in, chopped his left arm, and tipped him over. I held his
arm close to his body, reached down with my right hand, and
grabbed his wrist through his crotch. Mean. I cranked it back
toward me, and he moved wherever I wanted. I reached my
left arm across his face to hold him still while I pinned him
twenty seconds into the round.

In the championship, I faced a kid I had heard of. He was
a sophomore, and he won state as a freshman. This kid was

good—trained year-round, going to wrestling camps and probably gonna get a full ride to some Division I school in the Midwest. I couldn't place him in the state like the other kids. I'd never heard of his school before, Something Christian, and he looked like he had never been anywhere but on the wrestling mat. He was a blank slate. He was a true philosopher, a boy-king with a pale, round face and vacant blue eyes. He looked weak, no muscle definition, no scars or tattoos, but when I tried to move him, nothing happened. He didn't do anything in the first period, just figured me out, I guess. He didn't even smell like anything. I was starting to suck air from pushing so hard; I was sweating and getting worn out. I could see my coach yelling something in the corner of the mat, but I couldn't hear him. When the period ended and I walked over to him, he just said, "Hand control. Hand control."

In the second round, the kid was a bishop, a vicar of the wrestling gods, and I was some pagan getting converted in the desert—the cushy, dirty mat on the hardwood gym floor. He won the coin toss and deferred, and I took top. He blocked my leg easily and sat out so fast I didn't know what happened. He was a reflective surface; everything I threw at him, he just redirected, bounced, and channeled back into me. I was generating all the momentum of the match, and I was the one getting tired. Every time I pushed into him, I pushed myself. Every time I tried to force a turn or a move, I'd end up getting turned or moved. He was the real geometrician. In his heart, he possessed that ancient mathematic truth: that every triangle is just a piece of a circle. He was using sinusoidal functions, period waves, exposing the folly of my triangular thinking, flattening out the lines and curving them, introducing rates and change. He beat me into the laws of the holy unit circle, showed me how they govern every sharp angle. I was running from him, trying to catch my breath, but every angle I tried to cut away from him just radiated out to the curved edge of the ring.

In the third round, he put legs in on me. I was on my hands and knees, and his left leg was wrapped around mine, his ankle grabbing my shin like a hand. He faked like he was reaching for my right arm, so I immediately shifted all my weight to my left side. He baited me, and as soon as I took it, he moved left along with me and rolled me onto my back. Right when he flipped me, the whistle blew. I didn't know what happened, I hadn't been pinned, so I stood up confused.

He tech'd me, which is the wrestling mercy rule. If you beat the other guy by fifteen points, the match automatically ends. I hadn't even been paying attention to the points. He wasn't sweating. We shook hands, and the ref grabbed his wrist and lifted it. He didn't look at me or at anyone. He just walked over to his side and put on his pants.

We drove back from Jacksonville, and by the time we got home it was night. I heard about a party way down south of Gandy. It was a Sunday on a long weekend, and after I showered, I biked by the bay on my way there. My head was high chaos, and the night was loud with crickets. I looked out over the still black water as I biked and saw some gentle stirring out there, shark fins breaking the glassy plane. I put my bike up on the railing between the sidewalk and the bay. I looked out expecting to see some bonnetheads eating or fucking, little shovel-faced sharks like the ones my brother and I would catch off the bridge when we were kids. We would grab blue crabs off the barnacled walls and hook them as bait, and we'd catch sharks one after another, as easy as picking fruit. We would pull them out, and then he would put his hand to my chest and tell me to stand back while he finagled the hooks out of their mouths, those gloomy vacuums. He would wiggle the hook and avoid the hundred little sharp teeth around the rim. I would just stand and stare at their eerie alien skin, their gills pulsing fast, those exposed organs, those external lungs —creatures of a different world.

I wanted to call my brother, to mention the wrestling tournament but not talk about it, to talk instead about catching sharks. He loved fishing. He wrote his college application essay on the joys of quiet water, and it was good enough to land him a scholarship to some cold, landlocked school. I wanted to ask him if he missed it, if he wanted to come back for a bit, and when I got up on the railing, I saw it was a full moon and the low tide was lower than usual, and the blue crabs were sitting dumbly in the barnacles, and I wanted to tell him that there was plenty of bait, that they were hitting out there, ruffling the water. But we didn't have a relationship like that, really. I had his phone number, and he had mine, but we never used them. I looked out over the bonnetheads, but I saw they were actually a huge school of stingrays moving together; the sinewy, slippery wings cutting the surface of the water just looked like shark fins, and their bodies were tan like the sand, and they glowed in the streetlight, shone under the black water as they flopped on top of one another, swimming together like one giant sandpaper organism. Their slick figures were wet the way muscle probably looks wet under skin, steadily washed with blood. I thought about the hassle of catching a stingray, having to put a sandal or a shoe on the tail while you wiggled the hook out of their toothless maws, the way your bait would usually be hanging there, unchewed, just inhaled whole. The low tide stank, sulfurous and fishy, and I looked out over the water and the roiling stingrays, and I thought, *What the fuck has any of this ever done for me?* I spit one lazy strand of saliva off the seawall, and I fumed; the tidal waters of my heart pulled low, too, by the moon, exposing the barnacles that grew there, the hatred for the bay and school and wrestling and my family, my puny emotions. I hated everything I could see, north to south, east to west, everything I could set my mind on. I looked at the pink-gray clouds moving fast across the night sky, and I wanted to reach my hands up past them and pull the sky down on everything, to suffocate my little life and all the rest of the creatures that lived in the polluted bay. I wanted to see what was left, what was behind it all, what was so precious about any of this shit?

I picked up my bike and got away from that place as fast as I could — the bay, the moon, spooky and swampy, full of ghosts and monsters. I floated under the orange streetlamps, floated and floated, riding my anger like a current, I barely even had to pedal.

At the party, I meant to pick a fight with someone, but I

forgot. My ex-girlfriend was there, and I got drunk and tried not to look at her. I stole an Xbox from the guy whose house it was, and I bought some something, it's not important. Kicked the cycle into gear again, bender and release. I didn't wrestle another match, quit going to practice, and then school, for good.

5

I CAME TO ON the dirty carpet in a Walgreens, some cashier in a blue shirt kicking my foot. There's a bottle of keyboard duster in one of my hands and a drawstring bag in the other. The look on the guy's face is pure panic like I'm dead or something. My head's still got the wah-wahs, but they are fading now. I must have pulled the duster too hard while I was bent over and cut off all the oxygen to my brain and fell. The cashier starts to say something, but it seems like he can't decide what to say.

"What—"

"Do you—"

"Are you—"

I got up on all fours and ran past him and out the electric doors onto the street before he could figure it out. I look behind me, the cashier isn't following or even looking for me.

I have to play detective again, put it all together, under the pounding sun, inside my throbbing head — it's summer, summer and I think I'm at Hillsborough and Twenty-Second, miles away from my house, I'm wearing a bathing suit and an old pair of Nike running shoes with the shock absorbers at the bottom, but one of them is blown out, and it makes a squeaking sound as I walk. In my bag there's another T-shirt I don't recognize and a pair of boxer briefs; there's a fifth of tequila with a little gone and one of those fake lemons; there's a half-drunk bottle of promethazine and codeine and about twenty Xanax bars wrapped up in the cellophane from a cigarette pack; there is one blue in the plastic, too, and there's a cellophane-less pack of Marlboro Reds. In the little Velcro pocket of my board shorts, there's forty bucks and my phone and a lighter. My right hand is sore and fat, and it makes a clicking sound every time I open it. The knuckles are cut up. My nose is swollen and tender, underneath my eyes hurts, and I start to remember a big fight with my dad, my mom screaming at me and then at him as we start to get into it. I remember his knotty old hand cracking blood against my nose. I remember storming off, stealing money out of his wallet and her purse while my mom yelled at my dad, and he just sat there quiet and stubborn. Then she went quiet, and I remember leaving out the back door. I heard them as I left.

"I don't know what to do," she said, crying.

"What can you do?" he said, talking quiet the way he always did.

I walked down the street with my head tilted up, letting the blood run down my throat, coppery and rich.

* * *

But I couldn't remember how long ago that was, or what I had done in the meantime. Or how I ended up with twenty bars. I had a friend who lived right around where I was, so I called him to see if I could crash at his place for a little. He was a friend first, but he sold pills, and he was always flush with cash and whatever else. I'd known him since before he got into all that, but his parents were devout Muslims, so I knew I had to creep around his place when I was there. He made it real clear that they didn't have any tolerance for my type of shit.

"Yo, man, I'm right around the corner, can I come through and hang out for a bit? I need somewhere to chill."

"What?" he said over the phone.

"I just need to chill out for a few hours or something."

He went quiet for a second and said, "You've crashed here the past two days."

I didn't say anything.

"You just left an hour ago — you said you were gonna go get some food from the gas station."

"Oh," I said.

He started laughing. "You called me two days ago and said that exact same thing: 'I'm right around the corner.'"

I closed my phone and stared up at the loud sun. *It's summer,* I reminded myself. *You're seventeen.*

You guys gotta be gone by the time my parents get home.

I can't bring him back to my house. My mom is getting suspicious.

Doesn't he have a girlfriend? Can't he stay with her?

He already did that. He was doing that before he was with me.

I could hear them talking from the next room. I was in a bed kissing some girl I didn't know in a room I didn't know, someone's cousin from out of town or something, some relation to the girl whose house it was, I don't know. She was small and pretty, and her tongue was fat in my mouth, and it all tasted like tequila and lemon juice. She was moving her hand between my legs, and I went to do the same but my hand was throbbing, killing me, and it was starting to feel hot, and I wondered if I had a broken bone, and my vision started going, fuzzing up and then doubling, one image separating from itself and moving away fast, showing me a clone world in another dimension that disappeared and reappeared.

My parents are gonna come home and you guys can't be here.

I —

He's a fucking wreck.

I recognized the voice. It was a girl I knew from after-school treatment at the Phoenix House. We used to get high together, but she stopped and that must have been why she was so mad.

I sat up and I kissed her cousin soft, just with the lips, and I put my good hand on her stomach, then I took out my bag and grabbed the last few Xanax and put them in my swollen hand. I couldn't remember when the last time I took anything was, and, judging from the light peeking through the shades, it was somewhere in the afternoon. My board shorts were untied, and I stood up and asked, "Time is it?"

She said, "You just asked me that ten minutes ago."

I looked over at her.

"You sat up just like you are now, and you kissed me, and got out your bag, and took some pills and asked, 'What time is it?' You've done that three or four times already."

I said, "Doesn cousin, doesin have a pool?"

"What?"

I opened my mouth bigger and tried to move it more. "Doesn't your cousin have a pool?"

"Yeah, didn't you see it?"

"Let's go swimming," I said trying to sound out all the words.

"I don't know if you should get in the water right now," she said.

I smiled and said, "C'mon," and she smiled too.

"Can I have one?"

"One what?"

"One of those pills."

I looked at the four pills in my palm. They were long and green, and my hand was swollen and red, and I picked one up and gave it to her. She took out the tequila and washed it down and made a face. She passed it to me, and I did the same. She stood up, and I lay down and looked at her. She had long brown hair, and I dazed off a little staring at her.

She said, "What do these do, anyways?"

I tried to remember all that I knew they did. The little factoids from the drug forums, but my neurons were quiet and dumb and, when I tried to access them, through some positive to negative electric activity, I came up empty-handed.

"They're for anxiety," I said.

"You don't seem like the anxious type," she said. "Look away."

"What?"

"I'm getting into my bathing suit."

I faced the wall, and she said, "Are you always like this?"

"What do you mean?" The wall was a normal static color, but it was hypnotizing me, and I was really trying to hold on, so I could keep up the conversation, but my head and eyes were starting to get heavy.

"This fucked up. Are you always this fucked up?"

"I'm not sure," I said. "I doubt it."

She lay down next to me in her bathing suit and put her hand on the side of my face. It felt like, even with everything doubling and separating into different dimensions, it felt like I was really looking forward to something. That I was so happy about whatever was right around the corner, that whatever the next thing I was gonna do was, it would be amazing, and the excitement was physical and in my arms and my head and my stomach, and I felt like taking some more Xanax.

We kissed more and the time whittled away and all the Xanax I had forgotten I'd taken kicked in and rolled around through my veins, just laying waste to whatever was in there, growing bigger and more powerful and cleaning me out, until it got into my brain and wiped it out like an Etch A Sketch, and I came in and out of consciousness, and I couldn't remember who this girl I was kissing was, where I knew her from or where I was, but she was moving her hand in between my legs, and so I went to do the same to her but, whenever I moved it, my hand would start killing me. I sat up.

"Oh god," she said. "Not this again."

When I took out my bag, I couldn't find any pills, so I drank some of the cough syrup, and it was hot and sticky and my mouth was already dry, and she stood up and she said, "Let's go swimming."

And I noticed she was almost naked, she was wearing nothing but a little bit of string tied around her neck holding her boobs up in two nylon hammocks and a nylon loincloth around her butt, and I thought, *What is that, a bathing suit? How the hell did she get into a bathing suit?*

And she said, "What?"

It might have had little cartoon slices of watermelon on it, or it might have just been a pink and green suit, but then I noticed I was wearing a bathing suit too. She took my hand and led me outside.

There was a sliding door and a pool inside a screen cage, and I thought I must be in a gated community or something, which was kinda surprising, and I staggered out past the glass doors, and, as soon as the sun hit my eyes, it doubled and quadrupled and on, and it was at the perfect angle to hit the pool and turn it into something bright, some burning combination of all colors, condensed and powerful in its bright energy, and it contracted my pupils, and I went down, down onto the concrete with my head, my bathing suit loose and untied on my waist. And then the world came in even smaller snapshots —blood in my ear, ambulance, ambulance, hospital.

*   *   *

I was in the hospital, cold and small in the gown. Nicole was there, staring at me worried, and she must have called my mom, because my parents were there, staring at me worried.

I said, "What happened?"

They all looked at each other, and Nicole said, "You already asked that."

My parents were standing on opposite sides of the room, and Nicole came up closer to me in the bed, and I said, "I love you."

And she said, "Yeah, you already said that, too."

The catheter came out of its plastic package, and then it went in, and I was stuck there, tube in my dick. My mom came over and laid out some pieces of paper; information about rehab centers that accepted minors. Medical facilities, not like the behavior modification stuff I was used to. Science and pills and doctors. She looked at me, at the empty, static stupid in my eyes, all my diminished electricity, and she saw how little was going on in there, and she picked up the papers and put them back in their manila folder.

On the couch back home, I fell asleep for a day or so, and when I woke up, my mom was there with the papers again, and everything had worn off, and I looked at all the printouts — pictures of nice little clean places with pools and group rooms and beds and cafeterias.

I nodded, and the neurons started moving again, imbued

with some potential energy and aroused a pathway, created a little electric trail that manifested itself as a question: "Mom, I don't know what's happening to me."

And she started crying and I wanted to, too, but I was stuck on the verge, my eyes quivering but nothing falling, nothing fitting or resolving itself, just that question pathway, that electricity bouncing around like a Roman candle, over and over again: *What is happening to me?* I had a scream inside of me, but it wouldn't come out.

When I got there, they took my bag and put it on the bed and started leafing through it. The tech who was intaking me was in his mid-twenties, and he was telling me about the program and how he had gone there and been clean for a few years. He asked me what my drug of choice was. This was before I really got swept up in the crack and the speed.

"I don't know. Whatever, I guess. I'm not picky."

"Me too, man. Me too," he said. "I'm a garbage-head. Just throw whatever in there."

He inspected all the pockets in my bag and took out all my clothes and patted them down, and when he got to my bathing suit, he started laughing.

He held it up in the air, and he said, "Hey, Derek. Come here!"

Another young guy popped his head in the room and saw the bathing suit and started laughing too.

"You gonna go for a swim?" he asked.

"I thought there was a pool."

One of them said, "Oh yeah? Where'd you hear that, the website?"

They both laughed a little longer, and they laid the bathing suit flat out on the bed as they tossed my other stuff around.

I turned eighteen in there, and so I got some of my rights back. I became a patient instead of a ward, and as soon as that happened, on my birthday, I walked out the front door and away from the facility, down the street to a little public park with a playground, and I got on the swings. I swung from nine to five, like a job, all day, a birthday treat to myself. *Eighteen,* I thought, and I got into that pendulum motion, up and down, until I was totally hypnotized, with each swing a little bit of myself sloughed off, completely tranced until I couldn't remember my own name. Each push on the swing took me higher into space, into the future, eighteen years, at that vantage point I could look back on everything that preceded it, and then there was the sudden fall, giving me that lurch in my stomach, releasing something in my brain, endorphins or dopamine, something, a fraction of the exact thing I was trying to leave behind, the same hormonal language, little mock blips of protein binding to things in my brain, the hazy ghost of drugs.

When the day drew down, I slid my feet in the sand, and I was panting, sweating. I hadn't realized how tired I was, how thirsty from willing myself up into the air. I walked back to the facility smacking my parched mouth, trying to drum up some moisture, and when I got back it was all questions, drug tests, where'd I go, what'd I do? I was in trouble. They wanted to know if I got high, and I kinda did, but not in any way that shows up on a test.

"Can I have some water," I asked, "please?"

6

A BLURRY YEAR PASSED like miles of anonymous landscape, and suddenly I washed up into a scam rehab center
somewhere north of Boca Raton—one of those for-profit
places that has an army of lawyers who fight for money with
insurance companies all day. They weighed me when I got in,
106 pounds. I was still eighteen, and things were bad, but I
hadn't been to jail as an adult yet, and it hadn't been bad for
that long, and I was still using my mom's insurance, so things
must have been at least sort of all right. I had just got there, my
roommate a few days after me, and we were in a camera-moni-
tored detox room. He was an older guy. He shuffled in with his
bag and a lifetime of shit thoughts. He must have been in his
late sixties, and we didn't say a word to each other. He came in
late at night, and he lay in bed the whole next day. I watched
him walk in while I pretended to sleep. He slid his still-packed

bag under his bunk, like he wasn't planning on being there for long. He didn't get up for meals, and he didn't have any interest in getting to know me. I call him Walter in my mind, but I don't know if that was his real name. I don't think he ever actually told me. He was myopic in much the same way as I was. He was too busy reading the ticker tape of his own brain. All he did was lie in bed awake and shake, and from the shakes I figured he was there for booze. He only got up three times. The first was after a nurse roused him and made him go take his medicine. I watched him go to the nurse's window, and I peered into the tiny paper cup and saw two pills: lithium and phenobarbital, I thought. I was interested because I had been there a few days and everything was pretty much out of my blood and my head, and I was starting to miss it.

I was leaning against the wall, holding my pants up. They took away my belt, naturally, because I slipped up and told the truth when they were intaking me. They ask so many questions, it gets hard to keep track of when you should lie and when you should tell the truth.

So, Walter was taking phenobarbital; Walter was taking lithium. He was at the window, and he wanted more of the phenobarbital. He said last night they gave him more. Anger rose in him and then ebbed into passivity. He shuffled back into the room and went to bed. In a few hours, the nurse came in and gave him another dose.

The second time he got up on his own. The moment the clock hit six, he stood up and went to the nurse's window and got another dose. He looked worse than before; he looked like his mind was racing out of his eyes. His bag was still packed and under his bunk. He was wearing the same clothes as when he came in.

The third time, he sat up in bed and looked at me for a while. It was nighttime and I wasn't quite sleeping, but I was trying. The nurse had just come in and given him another dose, and after that he just stared at me for about fifteen minutes and walked to the bathroom to take a shower. Once he left, I sat up in bed, and I got out this applesauce cup that I pocketed from the cafeteria, and I peeled the foil lid off and folded it into a crude kind of spoon and shoveled the paste into my mouth. I had another one, and I ate that too. I flipped on the light and figured I would use the alone time to read and maybe it would put me to sleep. I only had the Big Book, so I opened that up and skipped the forewords and read "The Doctor's Opinion," which lays out the AA conception of alcoholism — a physical compulsion and a mental obsession. I read that whole chapter, and I skipped "Bill's Story" because I never really liked that part, and I got about halfway into "There Is a Solution," and I realized that he had been in the shower for a pretty long time. I could still hear the water running, and the bathroom doors in the monitored rooms don't lock, but it looked like he had propped something against it. Steam was coming out from the little eighth of an inch gap in the doorway.

I finished the chapter, and it must have been thirty minutes that he was in there, so I decided I would go and check on him. I knocked on the door twice and said "Hey," but I couldn't tell if he heard me. The water was loud, and the steam was so thick that it muffled the sound, and so I said,

"I'm coming in," and I pushed the door open, and saw a Bic razor on the ground with the sides busted off and the blade removed. He was lying there, and blood was still pouring out of his wrists, and it was puddled up under his ass and running in straight perpendicular lines through the grout lines around the tiles. I grabbed his wrists and put as much pressure as I could, and I kicked the door fully open and started screaming for help. A nurse rushed in, pushed me to the side, and switched places with me; she held his wrists and screamed for help, and another nurse ran in and they each bandaged a wrist, and someone called 911.

It must have been 120 degrees in that steamy room. I was sweating and Walter was drenched. His thin wet hair was stuck to his forehead, and his paunch and chest were glistening. His lips were blue, and his face was pale. I couldn't tell if he was breathing. I didn't want to look at his dick, so I just looked at my hands, which were smeared with bright blood. The nurses shuffled me out, and the paramedics showed up, then the cops, and I answered some questions, and they moved me to a different room. After I put my head on the pillow, I realized that I had forgotten to ask if he was alive or dead. I thought about this for a second before I slipped into the deepest sleep I had gotten since I'd been there.

I dreamt about the rain forest, foreign and strange. The lush green and the thick fog between the trees, the alien calls of monkeys and insects hooting and echoing around me. Everything was wet with mist. There were moist, dead logs, and trails of ants and beetles flowing in and out of the corridors of them, and it was so dim, but I could see little bits of light through the leaves as they danced.

A few days later, they called me into a room I hadn't been in before. It was a conference room with a big round table and a bunch of empty swivel chairs around it. There was only one person in there, a woman dressed in what looked like business clothes, a suit or a stiff dress, and she was wearing thick glasses. She told me to sit down, and she introduced herself and asked me some questions about how I was doing. I could tell she wanted to talk about the other night but was working up to it. I hadn't seen her around the treatment center at all, which I thought was strange because I had been there for about a week and felt like I had a pretty good handle on things.

When she brought it up, she didn't focus on the event, but she kept asking me how I felt about it now, if I was preoccupied with it, what had it been bringing up in me.

I told her the truth, "I'm fine," which is never good enough for a therapist or whatever she was.

She started to tell me about something called EMDR. "It is a form of therapy used to diminish negative emotions arising from unpleasant memories," she said. "Eye Movement Desensitization and Reprocessing."

She held out her index finger and said, "Focus on the finger," and I did, and then she said, "Focus on me," and we repeated this a few times to limber up my mind, to make it available and pliable.

She took out a small penlight and clicked it on. "Does this light bother you?"

I shook my head, and she asked me to get comfortable.

"Keep your palms open," she said. "Do not ball them into fists. You can rest them on your knees or on the table if that makes it easier. Look at my face."

She took off her glasses, and her face was calm, neutral. I couldn't read a single emotion or thought on it, and just looking at it made me feel relaxed. I started to feel the base of my skull tingle a little, and she held up the penlight and asked me to follow it around with my eyes. She moved it up and down, side to side, diagonally, all within a rectangle around her face and chest. She told me to just follow the light, to focus only on that for the moment. And as I did, I started to feel the edges of myself blur, I started to disappear into the fissures of my brain, and everything felt soft like my eyes were vibrating to some secret texture of the world.

She asked me to recall what I was doing before I found Walter.

"I was eating applesauce," I said, "then I was reading."

"And before that?" she asked.

"I was just lying in bed. The lights were off."

"Go back there," she said. Her voice was neutral too, light and soothing, and the tingling at the base of my skull was crawling down my neck and creeping into my shoulders. It felt like I had just gotten a haircut, and the breeze and the sun were taking turns tickling my neck.

"Think about the way the bed felt underneath you. Was it hard, was it soft? Think about the way the blanket felt on top

of you. Imagine the position of your body as best you can."
At this point, she started moving the light side to side only,
slow at first, but it was subtly gaining speed. I was following
it with my eyes, and I was losing a little bit of consciousness
with each movement. My eyes started to roll and I couldn't
focus; I drifted into the hardware of my mind, disconnecting
my vision from my brain, cutting through the practical pro-
gramming and taking me to some spaceless space, a purely
mental vacuum that exists only in the millions of molecular
shocks between my nerves, disappearing and reappearing in
different lobes and locations, and the space is empty at first
— nothing, then black, then white, then I was in the room, in
the bed. The bed was firm and the blankets were scratchy. I
could feel it on my skin.

"What is your roommate doing?"

"He is sitting up on the edge of his bed," I said.

"How does he seem?"

I am back in the room only I am sitting on the edge of Walter's bed, and I am looking over at myself in the other bed and
wondering if I am asleep. My hands are shaking from DTs,
and I wonder when the phenobarbital will kick in.

"Let the memory play out," she says. Her light is moving
back and forth pretty rapidly now and I am following it by instinct. For a second my eyes stray, and I wonder if I am ruin-
ing it by being Walter, should I tell her? Should I try to start
again?

My hands are shaking, and my bag is underneath me. I
have a weight on me, a lifetime of steady disappointments,
and my belly feels odd, the mass of it bunched up on itself

as I sit. I am right-handed now, only it doesn't feel strange. I am a plumber. I was a plumber. I get my shaving kit from my bag, and I take one last glance at the bed. I walk to the shower and turn it on. I close the door. I shove a towel underneath it and bunch it up to keep it closed. I take out the razor and start fumbling with it. I know how to do this, apparently. I remember prison. I remember a DUI, how hectic it was, the twisted metal and the sirens and lights from the ambulances and the cop cars. I break the bottom plastic off, but my hands are shaking so bad it takes a while, and I nick myself. I start working on the pieces of plastic on the sides. I take deep breaths to steady myself, and the room, as it fills with steam, is becoming suffocating. I can feel the lack of oxygen in each breath. I am weak but driven. I start to bite at one of the sides; I cut my lip, but I keep going. I crack the plastic away, and I start to push the exposed blade. I bend it; I remove it, and I look at the glass of the mirror. I wipe it. I watch the clear part of the glass fog back up, and I think, *This is the last time I will ever see glass fog over,* and I look at my legs, hairless and pale, and think, *This is the last time I will ever have a body,* and I take off my boxers to look at the rest of it.

I sit on the toilet, and I slide the razor over my skin. The blade is thin and hard to grip; my blood is loose and runny from the heat and the moisture, and as it spills into my hand, I start to lose a sense of where the blade is. I get worried and I push harder. I switch hands, and blood from my left wrist starts dripping on to my right and mixing with the newer blood that beats out as I rake the razor. I am worried that not enough blood is coming out, so I start to saw at it. The plastic toilet seat is slippery and so are my legs and my thoughts, and I see lights pop and disappear at the top of my line of sight. I slide off the toilet, and I lie on the tile, staring up at the light fixture and watching the steam swirl in front of it. I watch the new, thick fog billow from the shower and run into the lighter mist on top of me. I lie there and feel myself flowing out like a snaked drain — like an old hairy clog had finally been removed. I lie there until I hear knocking. I brace myself for what I know is coming, as I drift into unconsciousness, into the place where everything is bright. Then I bust through the door and lurch back into my own body, and the therapist must be able to sense that this is the bad part because she says, "Focus back on the light."

And I do. I see the light again, moving metronomically across her body, and she says, "Think, and I know this is difficult, but try to think of something positive, something pleasant to replace this with. The first thing that comes to mind."

And I am back in the bathroom, yellow and hot, and I hear the water in the shower like the rustle of trees and the droning of birds, and I am in the jungle from my dream. It is green, it is hot, and the sun is shining through the dancing leaves. The steam is the jungle mist, and his body is the rotten log. For a moment, the scene oscillates between these two places. It flickers rain forest and bathroom, and when I see his body I rush to grab it, to cover his wrists, and then it shifts back to the log, and I am trying to cover the empty caverns, and the ants and beetles are crawling over my hands, marching in perpendicular lines and trying to fight their way in and out of the fragile wood.

I am sweating in the conference room, and my jaw is sore. My hands are balled into tight fists, and my forearms ache from exhaustion. She slows the light down a little to bring me back, and she says, "You saved his life, you know?"

"No, I didn't know."

"His wife asked us to thank you."

"I didn't really know what I was doing," I say.

"Even so."

I wonder if Walter is mad at me for what I had done. Whether I would occupy some kind of singular place of hatred and regret in his mind. Someone who blocked his exit, who stole his last opportunity. I feel a strong need to apologize to him. To write him a letter and say: *I didn't mean to. I wasn't thinking. I'm sorry, man. Try again, and I won't do anything, I promise.*

"It usually takes about eight sessions to properly reprocess," she says. "We can do twice a week for the rest of your treatment." I don't want to, but I nod anyways. I refuse the next time they ask me to go, and I leave treatment about a week later.

7

NINETEEN, ANOTHER MONUMENT, and it was an-
other hot January, a few days after New Year's, and I was on
the street staring at a sheer wall of words printed on T-shirts
in a shop window in Delray Beach, people walking past me
up and down Atlantic Ave. I was smoking a purple 305 and
grinding my teeth while the snowbirds popped in and out of
the shops and the loud restaurants around me.

The shirts said:

DON'T TALK TO ME UNTIL I'VE HAD MY COFFEE
FUCK YOU, THAT'S WHAT
FLUENT IN SARCASM
A T-shirt with a weed leaf
A sweatshirt with Obama and Tupac
A sweatshirt with Obama in a turban

I was broke, and the girl I had been running around with had just gotten arrested and, all of a sudden, I didn't really have a place to stay anymore, didn't really have anything to do.

She was over at some halfway house where the manager sold dope, and everyone who lived there bought it from him. She was tricking, and I was pretty much just mooching off of her and doing odd jobs for the guy who ran the place. I was sleeping on the beach, and I was sandy all the time. I had gotten crispy and lost my trash bag full of clothes. I hadn't been back to Tampa in a year, and I hadn't talked to anyone who knew me in about as long. I was anonymous, one of those shapeless phantoms that slides around the periphery of crack houses with no past and no future.

Looking at all the shirts in the window, I wasn't exactly missing her, but I was bored, and I wished she was there. Alone, I can start to get weird.

A few hours before, I was smoking crack laced with PCP, and I left 'cause I was broke, and so I went out to Atlantic to see what I could pull. The crack had worn off, but the PCP was still going, and I was flirting with that out-of-body camera — T-shirts, me at the window, T-shirts, me at the window — in and out.

There was a guy I recognized from somewhere, maybe rehab or some job I used to have, playing sad songs on his guitar on the sidewalk, up against the wall with his case open. He looked so foolish, playing gloomy music against all the happy tourists, but the song started to get to me and mess with my head, changing the way I saw the scene unfolding. The people out having fun on that thin street looked like they were just going through the motions, myself included, like none of us actually wanted to be here, like we were just milling around compulsively. I nodded to him while he played, and he nodded back, could probably tell by my grinding teeth what was going on with me, where I was headed, and what I was doing.

I could see the words on the T-shirts being stamped and printed on my brain, in their same all-caps font.

LIFE'S A BEACH

IT'S 5 O'CLOCK SOMEWHERE

MASTER BAITER

And I was confused. The words on the shirts started to coalesce and harden into the boundaries and unspoken assumptions of my thoughts. They formed the outer reaches of the linguistic world I lived in; they were the world's physical laws. I had a pen in my pocket and a napkin, and I wanted to jot all these T-shirt slogans down, copy them, and go somewhere to decipher their messages. And as I started to move to do it, to reach into my pocket, I got a little ahead of myself, and I put the napkin up on the window, which was wet with condensation from facing the hot night, and my pen ripped the damp paper, but I got a couple of phrases down, some crude sketches, and as I felt the paper lose integrity, I realized I was still reaching for my pen. That I hadn't even touched it in my pocket yet. I turned around quick to see if anyone had noticed what happened, if anyone could remind me what I was reaching for.

* * *

I watched the people go by a little more intently. It must have been a Saturday because the streets were crowded with Bermuda shorts and blotchy, red skin. I watched and analyzed their wardrobes, calculating costs in my head, looking at jewelry, shoes, and purses. People were staring back at me, a crazed and crooked figure leaning against the wall, uncomfortable and empty-pocketed, with a clenched and gaunt face, black rings under wild junkie's eyes. They would glance briefly and, when they saw me looking back, avert their eyes and focus hard on keeping them averted. But they always looked again, once or twice, against their better judgment, an activated animal instinct for awareness and self-preservation even in these most comfortable of creatures.

There was someone who looked like me, only older, softer, and more grounded, walking the street quizzically, examining things like a surveyor, judging the slope of the street and counting the heads of pedestrians. He held a notebook under his arm, a pen behind his ear, and had a squint on his face of pure scientific observation, and behind the squint, if I saw it right, melancholy, nostalgia, or perhaps just recollection. I watched him for a little bit and then moved on to others.

A woman and her husband left one of the shops and started walking toward where I was. She was putting her wallet into her purse. It had no handles, just one thin chain that hung limply down as she held it by the body. It was Louis Vuitton, and I could tell by her shoes and her earrings that it wasn't fake. I started walking toward them, looking beyond them as if aiming to go past.

The street like a long hallway, and the T-shirts in the window hanging like art on the walls. The comedown was starting to bang against my brain.

She was on the inside, and her purse was too. I hung close to the wall. She stirred a deep hatred inside of me, a measurable feeling of destructive energy. I wanted everything she had. I wanted to leave her naked and confused in the street. I wanted her to feel the terror of my comedown; I wished I could cough it onto her like a contagion, to wipe the dumb happiness from her face, replace it with sick horror, mad loneliness.

Unconsciously, instinctually, even within the hazy lines of PCP streaking across my brain, I judged our speeds, my footsteps and theirs, held them up to the unheard metronome in my internal clock, whatever that true, objective measure of time is, not seconds or man-made minutes, but the one that beats along to life in the brain stem. Timing the sounds of movement with the image of them growing larger, all these little involuntary exercises of perception and judgment, the instinctual understanding of being in the world. How long for ten steps to turn to five, to two. There was sand in my Air Maxes; it was interfering with my steps, making them slide instead of striking the ground resolutely; it was throwing me. And at three steps, I dropped my cigarette onto the sidewalk under where my right foot would be in the next moment. They watched this, and at one step I glanced to the woman, passing my right shoulder not to her exactly but to the height and distance of the purse in relation to me. I turned my shoulder just a little, enough to use my right arm as insurance against the purse getting away, and I reached over quick with my left hand and grabbed it; it slipped out of her hand easily. She was holding it with no care or awareness, and I angled my right shoulder forward hard, to shift my momentum, as I broke into a run, she yelled, and people turned, and I took the first corner as some of them started to chase me. I looked back to see how many there were, and I counted three, and I saw the guitar guy's face, smiling from where he was sitting on his overturned paint bucket, the guy who looked like me still scribbling in his notebook, watching with cold stillness.

I ran through a parking lot, and I hit the next gear. I put a little bit of space between me and the people chasing, and I threw the purse into a bush at the base of an oak tree in the middle of the lot. I ran a block and turned left and then did it again. I knew this was the most important part because if I could hit that second turn before they could make the first, then I'd be gone. I pushed it as hard as I could. Despite the sand shifting in my shoes, the fear made me faster than whatever was driving them. I did it by a fraction of a moment. Now that they couldn't see me. I kept running, fifteen seconds, made a couple random right turns, and I jumped behind a hedge that butted right up next to a one-story brick building.

I lay there in the mulch, parallel to the hedge and the brick wall, and I tried to arrest my breathing, to make it quiet. I listened as they yelled to each other, but my heart was so loud in my ears that I couldn't make out what they were saying.

I remembered a game of manhunt when I was a kid. Me and two other neighborhood kids hiding while my brother and some others looked for us. It was Christmastime, the whole neighborhood at our disposal. There was a house with an old plastic manger scene decoration in the front yard, and the owners had painted the glowing baby Jesus a deep brown. On our head start, I got one of the kids on my team to lend me his shirt. I knelt down with the plastic wise men, and I wrapped the shirt over my head. I knelt there as still as I could, grass pushing red indentations into my knees. I closed my eyes, and I held my hands to my face like I was praying to the newborn Jesus. I remembered wanting to laugh as I heard my brother and the other kids walking by, looking everywhere for me. I had to go somewhere in my mind to keep from doing it, so I pretended I really was a wise man. I went to the desert, to the starry Palestinian sky, and I followed a shooting star in my mind. I pretended I was leading a donkey and hiking over dunes of loose orange sand, slipping and striding along in a trail of pack animals, hiking for so long that I couldn't distinguish between myself and the donkey, lost into the collective consciousness of like-minded animals. I thought about following a star, of being dragged behind it like a comet's tail, trailed for miles, happily unaware of where I was being led. I thought about the gifts: gold, frankincense, and myrrh. I imagined them in an expensive purse, snug in an exotic leather pouch. I was full of hope, faith in the new life born at the end of the trail, at the spot where the star smashed into the Earth. Nobody found me.

I could hear my brother saying, "The game's over. We give up."

I could hear him saying to his teammates, "He's such a little freak. He could be anywhere."

I was starting to get bored, and I had exhausted my imagination in the desert, had made it to the manger already and seen what I came to see. So, as soon as I heard my brother pass, I jumped up and bolted for "base."

In the hedge, after I had used up the manhunt memory, I started to think about the purse. I leafed through it in my mind: a wallet stuffed with cash, $500 sunglasses, credit cards, iPhone, and expensive makeup. The bag itself worth probably $1,000 new, but I'd have to convince whoever I sold it to that it wasn't fake or listen to them try to convince me that they thought it was. I could maybe sell it for a hundred bucks. I started to feel restless again, to feel the absence of the crack like phantoms in my veins. The voices had died down, but I knew it wasn't time to leave yet. I tried to imagine a map in my head of where I was in relation to the purse and the spot where I grabbed it. I zoomed out and drew Atlantic Ave. first, running east–west, then I put the Intracoastal and Swinton Ave. as my boundaries. I marked the police department and the courthouse and the library west of Swinton, the beach east of the Intracoastal. I marked the Starbucks and the Mexican restaurant where the guy was playing Neil Young on his paint bucket. I found the spot where I grabbed it, and I found my first cross street. I found the angle I took through the parking lot and the tree where I dropped the purse, then I traced my first left turns and then the others, found out I was right up against Swinton a few blocks south of Atlantic. I knew I just had to cross Swinton to get to a dealer. I started getting butterflies thinking about it, felt my mouth water and my heart rate pick up again.

My plan was to wait thirty minutes, but I completely lost track of time. It could have been ten minutes or an hour, I didn't know, but I couldn't sit still anymore. I was just thinking about crossing Swinton over to the Haitian neighborhood where guys stood out by the street, pockets stuffed full of crack and blues, waistbands pulled tight around pistols. I imagined my good mood, that feeling of anticipation, chopping it up with the dealers using all ten words of Creole that I knew. I hadn't heard anything in a minute, so I figured it was probably clear. I just needed to make it a few blocks, anyways.

I went back to the parking lot, warily at first but my mind kept coming back to copping and loading the stem and twisting it around in my fingers, holding the flame and drawing in long and slow. I bent down at the base of the oak, and as soon as I touched the bag, the red and blue lights flipped on behind me. I planted my right foot and took off for a side entrance of the parking lot, but another cop car pulled right in front of me, and I tried to turn on another burst of speed, but I was tapped out. My legs were gone, jelly from no food, no sleep, and all that running. He put me down in the middle of the street, and I felt my face scrape against the gravel and the asphalt, little pieces of grit and sand diffusing into open skin. His knee was in my back with his full body weight, and he must've been over two hundred pounds because it felt big and heavy, final. He bent my arms back until the joints hurt and put the cuffs on me tight.

"Where were you headed, big guy?" he asked.

I didn't say anything.

He pulled me up off the ground and bent me over the trunk of the car. I felt all the fatigue of sleepless days hit me at once. The prospect of crossing Swinton gone in an explosion of inevitability and shame.

He started patting me down and asked, "You have any weapons?"

I shook my head.

"Anything that could stick me?"

"No."

"Anything at all you want to tell me about?"

I shook my head again.

He ran my pockets and took out the McDonald's napkin with ten digits scrawled on it and the pen with no cap.

"That's it? That's all you got?"

"I thought I had cigarettes," I said. "I don't know where they went."

He took off my shoes one by one and ran his hands in them, feeling only sand.

"Christ. What d'you live at the beach?"

My shoulders throbbed, my wrists ached, my face stung, and my legs were completely numb. I noticed how thirsty I was; I couldn't remember the last time I'd had a sip of water. I couldn't really make out his face. It was dark, and I still hadn't caught my breath, every trace of every drug was gone now, and I was in pure lack. My head felt like a stubbed toe. He was big with a big cop head, like a grouper or a pit bull, I tried to focus on him or read his badge, but it was useless.

He read me my rights. "With these rights in mind, do you wish to speak to me?"

"Yeah, what the hell."

"So, what happened here?"

I was watching the second cop unpack the purse, and inside the purse was a wallet that looked just like it, brown with *LV*s all over it. He opened it up and pulled out three hundred-dollar bills and a bunch of twenties.

"Some people travel heavy, huh?"

He laid the bills out on the white trunk, and I stared at them hungrily.

"What were you gonna do with all this cash?"

"What do you think?" I said.

"You were gonna buy flowers for your boyfriend?"

I stared at him.

"Don't worry, you'll have plenty of boyfriends soon."

I tried to think of something to say back. Cops always think they're funny, and they think they can freak you out, and I guess they were right because I didn't have anything but shame in my stomach, passing through my veins into my head like a regular drug. All of my abstractions melted away. I felt like a normal person again in the worst possible way. Aware of consequences, of reality and fear. I was thrust back into the supervision of normal people, people who ate breakfast and dinner, who laughed at the same jokes and held the same things dear. I hated this part more than anything. The lights on the car were still on, revolving red and blue.

"You know anything over three hundred dollars is a felony, right? Five years minimum."

The other one piped up, "How did you know she was gonna have so much cash? Lucky guess?"

"Were you following her?"

I clammed up, and they stuffed me in the car and drove me to county. I was trying to kick my mind into gear, to get it to race again, to think of something, some way out of this shit, but it was empty.

In the car, the lectures started — the moral high ground, the horror stories, and the tales of redemption.

In booking, at first, it was just me and another kid my age sharing the big yellow room with benches on either side. He was an ugly, weaselly looking kid with bad tattoos and holes in his ears for gauges. He didn't have the gauges in, and the lobes of his ears were swollen and infected, puckered and yellow and purple. Looking at them made me nauseous, so I tried to look away when he talked.

"Those shoes are sick," he said.

I ignored him and lay out on the bench. I tried to look out the vertical windows on either side of the big steel door, the glass thick and latticed with safety wire. Outside just looked like a hospital or some anonymous office, the only difference being that everyone was in a cop's uniform. I could feel all the muscles in my back and my legs tightening up, sore from withdrawing. My face was still stinging and starting to itch, and as bad as I wanted some crack, I realized I wanted a cigarette more.

As the hours of the night grew larger and then receded, more and more people were brought in. We got taken out one by one, fingerprinted and strip-searched and examined by the nurse and then returned like a library book. She put some paste on the edge of a long Q-tip and rubbed it onto the cut on my face. It burned, but it concretized the pain at least. She scribbled *topical Bactroban* onto my paperwork.

When I got back, the spot where I had been lying on the bench was taken, and I had to squeeze in somewhere else. The room was starting to stink with bodies, bodies from different neighborhoods and families with their different smells, doing different things, skin holding and excreting different chemicals — body odor and booze, the lingering smears of strip club body butter, dust and drywall from jobsites, smoke and cheap cologne and unwashed dick, unbrushed teeth. Just as it was getting crowded and loud, someone got up and started taking a shit on the little metal toilet in the corner of the room. Everyone yelled at him, and he was yelling back. He was big enough that nobody would do anything about it, and it was booking, so it wasn't even real jail, and no one wanted to fight, but the yelling was a necessary step. No one in there was a stranger to this phenomenon, the communal toilet, but they yelled anyways, sticking up for whatever lingering dignity they had. Getting popped makes your nerves go wild, makes your stomach speed up, but even still, there was something too primal about it, this man squatting and shitting four feet away from us. It was too uncivilized. It was something, subconsciously and without articulation, we were all told we were better than as a species. The days of indiscriminate animal shitting were supposed to be over. We were supposed to have evolved beyond that.

The noise was overwhelming me, and I put my hands over my ears, and I closed my eyes and laid my head back against the painted cinder-block wall. I tried to will all of my senses off — sight and sound and smell and taste and touch. I tried to separate the ghost that lives in my body, to coax him out and walk him through the wall and out of the building, to fly him up over the highway and out back to the beach, or maybe farther, out into the ocean, vast and insensitive, the desert of timeless space. But my imagination was dead, and I couldn't even feel my ghost. I was just body, mortal and material, one sensory organ, feeling and smelling and hearing, decomposing a little bit every second.

I took off my shoes and turned them over, pouring the sand out onto the tile floor. My feet felt much better in the shoes, had some room to breathe, the curves of my toes falling into their assigned indentations. I realized I was sweating even though the room was freezing. I was sweating from fear, which was crowding the inside of my heart. I started to notice all the faces in the room, how close they were to mine, how scared of them I was. All of the unknowns. The unknown people and the unknown place, unknown where I was going next, for how long. And the scariest unknown of all, how I got there, the purse and the cop car purged from my memory; I couldn't remember a room before this one, before the open toilet and the scary, ugly company; their eyes beaming thoughts into my head, *Who the fuck is this kid, why is he acting so strange,* their heads nearing mine every second, tilting in and getting closer and closer, stifling my sense of self, making me even more discrete, hardening the outline of my being but shrinking it every second.

8

I TRIED TO GET BACK ON my medication, but they didn't have the XR capsules in county, so they just gave me the same dose but regular release. The pills were hitting me too hard and making my stomach feel light and my head feel heavy. At first, I thought it was just withdrawal, but they stuck around, and I was getting brain zaps — little shocks on the side of my head and down through my jaw like I was being tased randomly throughout the day. It all took less than a second, but my eyes would shut tight and a flash of light would pop on the side of my head. They put me on some other shit, too — Risperdal, the anti-psychotic that stayed on me like a weighted blanket, and some pill that they said would stop the involuntary movements in my arm that were a side effect of the Risperdal, but it didn't work. Anyways, they all slogged together in my bloodstream, and I woke up feeling like I had sandbags tied to my neck.

After a few months of waiting, the judge had hung the ax over my head, given me time served, and sent me to Avon Park, to the Florida Center for Addictions & Co-occurring Disorders. Sitting chained together in the courtroom with all the other guys who had hearings that day, I saw the young lawyers, public defenders milling around, only a few years older than me, it seemed. They put us in our own little compartment to the front and side of the courtroom, in front of all the people with jobs, and no one so much as glanced at us. When it got to my name on the docket, the judge told me to stand. My lawyer said some stuff, the prosecutor said some stuff, and the judge turned to me and told me I got lucky.

He said, "Don't ever let me see you in my courtroom again." I reached down to that bottommost part of my stomach, where I stored all my truest sentiments, where I held the things I meant and believed, and I assured him that he wouldn't. And in that moment, I did mean it, and I believed it, and I wanted nothing more than for it to be true.

They put me in a paddy wagon and drove me up through the Everglades, right past Lake Okeechobee through all that Seminole land, and took me to some truck-stop town off Highway 27, right to the absolute middle of the state. It occurred to me that I had never stayed anywhere this far from the water. Landlocked. Flat endless land. Lowland.

"You ever been to Highlands County?" one of the cops turned back and asked me.

"No."

"You're gonna love it," he said.

I looked out through the tiny hole in between them and me, covered in metal mesh, so I could see through the windshield. That dead-looking yellow grass covering geometric miles, like some kind of pesticide had been sprayed down from the sky.

I hadn't been in a car in at least a year, excluding the cop car that brought me in and the city bus and the sheriff's department bus that took me to the courthouse chained up to all the other sad fucks. And I hadn't seen anything except Gun Club for the past few months. It felt strange to be moving so fast, covering so much ground. It felt good for a while and then it didn't. I couldn't look out the window anymore because I thought I was about to throw up. My fingers tingled from the cuffs, and my hands were hanging down chained loosely to my feet. My legs started to cramp too. But it felt good to be out of jail. It felt real good. To not be crowded, to not have to listen to the chatter and the COs.

At my feet was a paper bag with my belongings. When I was arrested, I was just wearing a T-shirt and a pair of black jeans, and when the cops searched me, I only had that pen and the McDonald's napkin in my pocket. Luckily, my crack pipe and my rig were under a rock in an alley somewhere; I had lost a sweatshirt but bought a hoodless gray one in jail by selling my medication. I was wearing that under my blues, and I had managed to keep my shoes, which, in spite of everything, were actually still in pretty good shape. The gray-and-black Air Max 90s. I had tried them on in a Foot Locker a few weeks before I got popped. I walked out the door in them, then ran out of the mall and into a bus and rode back across town. If I hadn't gotten picked up, I probably would have ended up trading them at some point.

When they pulled me out of the back of the van, the cop handed me the paper bag and said, "I don't know whose dick you had to suck to end up here instead of up the road. But you oughta consider yourself lucky."

The hallway, the linoleum floor — all-white, government tile with random colored ones peppered in like stepping-stones across a shallow river. I saw a guy I knew from back in Tampa, Fernando, sitting at a little school desk in the hall, cuffed up and staring at his Nikes. He was as short as ever, but he had put on weight since the last time I'd seen him. He looked meaner like he had been working out too much, and we didn't acknowledge each other as familiar, but as I walked by I asked, "Where you going?"

And he said, "Back."

The two cops who drove me came over to him and took him outside and loaded him into the van. I was happy he was gone. I didn't feel like knowing anyone.

In intake the nurse took my blood pressure and asked me a bunch of the usual questions. About my vaccines and my drug use, the tuberculosis test I got and the infected burn on my arm that had been festering while I was in jail. She was sweet and clumsy, sweeter than the nurses in county, but I got the feeling that she would rather be talking to anyone in the world except me. I felt like I was at the vet, and she was making sure I had my shots and checking me for worms, fleas, ticks. She wouldn't look me in the eyes. She just examined me and looked at my papers. When she took my blood pressure, her fingers grazed me for a second, and I flinched a little and got chills at the back of my head that ran soft electric down my arms. I realized I hadn't been touched in a few months, not since my last fight when I first got in. I tried to hold on to that soft electric feeling, to see if I could make it stay on the back of my neck for the rest of the day, but it went away after she ripped off the Velcro cuff. It returned when her stethoscope touched my back, when her fingers were on my wrist, and it went away again when we got back to the questions.

She only looked me in the eyes after we went over my sexual history: protection, partners, how many, men, women, have I paid, have I been paid, how long. She asked me about needles and sharing them, and she got out some pamphlets about HIV and hep C and really started to lay into me. She didn't seem sweet anymore, the little pink oval of her mouth spitting numbers and rates and responsibility. She tied a thick rubber band around my bicep while she was talking, but I couldn't hear her anymore. All I could hear were the veins in my arms getting fat and the needle in her hand. The sharp, clean needle. My heart was beating faster and moving up my throat, throbbing into my ears, and I couldn't wait a second more for her to stick me. My mouth was watering, and I thought I could even taste a little metallic breeze on the sides of my tongue. She hit me like a pro and my knees went weak, but then I remembered that she was just taking blood and not giving me anything.

She said, "You'll be lucky if this comes back negative."

•   •   •

Breakfast was at seven, and I never felt like eating. At 8:15, we shuffled into the group room for exercise. It was like every other room in the place, highly uniform, only all of the chairs were pushed back toward the wall in a hurry, not stacked or in rows, but just kind of shoved away at angles and in clusters. They cleared the space for Richard Simmons. They would put in a DVD of *Sweatin' to the Oldies* and make us dance.

"Are you ready?" Richard would ask.

"Okay!" he would answer.

And with slow, medicated arms, I would half-assedly try to follow. Like the chairs, we were in no particular order, no rows or lines, but there was a certain logic to it. The younger guys and I in the back, this music and this dancing an affront to everything we thought we stood for. The guys who didn't think about it or didn't care were in the middle, just another hoop to jump through — they understood the nature of these institutions. And then, some of the guys who seemed to genuinely enjoy it, they were up front, trying to get their heartbeats up, listening to the music and letting it in.

"Great Balls of Fire," "Proud Mary," "California Dreamin'," "It's My Party," "Dancing in the Street," "Hit the Road Jack," "Mony Mony," "Big Girls Don't Cry."

Dwight was an old crackhead from Lakeland. He was apparently a high school football star back in the eighties, but now he only had one leg. The other one was cut off at the knee, and he had a metal prosthetic that I could hear squeaking while he was dancing. He would get so into it. He would answer all of Richard's questions and copy all his moves until he was actually pouring sweat in that little tile group room, in front of that fat, old TV.

They assigned me to Dr. Greg. An overweight, jolly shrink who wore his pants up by his belly button. He showed me a trick once; he said, "Tell me your three earliest memories, and I can show you how you have been replaying those narratives for your whole life." He said he could establish patterns built on these basest memories.

When I was four, I was at the playground with my brother. He and his friends were chasing each other and climbing around on the jungle gym. I was climbing, too, in my young and slow way. Trying to keep up. I was climbing the ladder to the slide, and my hand slipped on one of the rungs. The side of my head smacked one of the bars as I fell, and I broke my skull before I landed in the soft sand. It was loud in a way that only I could hear, like a shotgun blast, bright and sudden. My mother ran over to me in mute panic. She put me on her hip to take me to the hospital, and I rested my head on her shoulder, still reeling from the bang. I looked at the fabric of her dress on her shoulder and I started to feel sick. Even though it's my first memory, I must have earlier ones because I remember that it was my favorite dress that she had. She wore it often, and when I think of her as she was when I was little, she is wearing it. It was white with little pink and green flowers; they were simply drawn like a cartoon almost, pretty and neat in little rows. The colors and the predictability of the pattern made it so pleasing to me. There must have been hundreds of the little flowers arranged like that across her back, and now the symmetry of it all was making me even more nauseous, spreading out and surrounding me. I was trying not to throw up, not to throw off the balance of the neat little rows, but I did, all across her chest and arms.

"Are you still mad at yourself for spoiling her dress?" he asked me.

"I don't know, I hadn't thought of it until now," I said.

I can't remember where I heard it, but somewhere I got the idea that human beings had become smart because of our dexterity. That our fingers' ability to do fine movements made us smarter over time and made our fingers even better, even more capable of even finer movements and thus smarter still. Our brains grew fatter and more powerful, like each finger movement was a flex of the mind.

I hadn't been using my body at all. It had just been sitting there: idle, tired, relaxing into puddles. I thought about the way I was living before — using coins to unscrew the hoods of air conditioners, unspooling copper wire, a fine two-finger pinch to slide a wallet out of a pocket, the palming of a candy bar off a rack, opening batteries, gauging coke, crushing Sudafed, tablespoons and half cups, little bits of powders and crystals, dripping water into the basin of a spoon, removing a filter from a cigarette, manipulating twenty-gauge needles, watching for air, finding a vein, ripping tiny pieces of Brillo, jamming them in narrow stems, taking safeties off of lighters, and measuring flames. Steady, always steady and always minute, fastidious detail. Technical movements.

And yet, too stupid to know how to keep a job. How to finish school or stay out of trouble.

I decided I would start off basic. Basic movement of the arms and legs. Running. I hadn't done it since the cops and, before that, maybe to catch a bus. Running. I went out to the patch of grass by the fence. I marked a spot by the chain-link. I laid my shirt out in a line across the grass. Wind sprints. A phrase I remembered from a life before. The end of wrestling practice. Everyone tired, mad, cracking jokes. The coach standing, goading, blowing his whistle. Maybe a punishment.

There and back. Plant the foot, bend down, touch the shirt, pivot, and return. Once. I'm gassed. Twice. My lungs are full of dry ice. My thoughts are short like my breath. Halfway through the third, I give up and put my hands on top of my head. I lie on the grass and watch imaginary flecks of light pop and swing and disappear. I feel my heart against my rib cage and my arm tingles and goes numb. Two and a half sprints, maybe a tenth of a mile. My throat is dry and scratched like I've been running in the cold but it's eighty degrees out.

Before bed, I try push-ups. Sit-ups. I think about my dad. Always twenty, until it was fifty, until it was fifty and fifty again. I think about "enrichment." Watery eyes and a thick hand. A wedding ring cracking my cheekbone. Left-handed, a southpaw in baseball and boxing. Him watching me as I pressed down to the unforgiving ground, hard and cold and still. He would watch to make sure I touched the tip of my nose to it, that I didn't bend my back or legs, that I was making the task as difficult as it could be. Completely parallel. He told me that my grandfather was a bricklayer. Bricks, concrete, marble, and tile. Anything stone. He would say this with reverence, the way dads talk about old things from the past. With pride or respect or maybe even fear, some lingering fear from when he was a kid, because laying bricks meant his hands were strong and heavy, that they carried some weight when they found you. And it meant his forearms were used to pushing, to pulling, and another person was light compared to what they were used to doing. *And he was precise,* my dad said, *everyone who ever worked with him hated him because he wasn't afraid of starting over from scratch.* He wasn't afraid of perfection like some people. His understanding of a straight line was 180 degrees — *straight meant straight to him,* my dad said, *and to see it mean something else, "straight enough," to the world, drove him crazy,* so crazy that it bled through generations and drove me crazy, definitely drove my old man crazy. *The world needed people like him,* my dad said, like us, to spend all day flattening the ground until it's straight, to never draw a line without a ruler. Who else was gonna make sure the houses wouldn't fall down, wouldn't crumble in the rain, that the floor and the foundation would be level, that life could occur on solid ground. My dad would point to houses and offices all around town that my grandfather worked on, still standing nice and straight, six, seven decades, like nothing of consequence had ever happened in all those long years. Resolute and ready to stand for more decades, centuries if they had to, and if the whole rest of the city got eaten back into the world, they would still be there, monuments to his single-minded hatred of crookedness, to the man who refused to give a millimeter to erosion, or friction, or moisture, or whatever other slight worldly forces steal energy from human projects over great stretches of time.

And that's what I would think of while doing push-ups. The ground, level and rigid, how I had to stay parallel to it. How touching my nose and chest to it was some kind of ancestral ritual, prayer to the God of Straight Lines. And in that moment, on the floor of the open dorm, I harbor only the deepest love for my father for doing this for me, doing it not out of sadistic pleasure or frustration but out of duty. I bring my lips to the ground when I do my push-ups, I kiss that which holds me. Discipline was prayer to him, every bit as loving and necessary, that feeling tangible in the air while he watched me do my push-ups, shot into me between breaths, the same dutiful gaze I would see when he sat me and my brother in the backyard and gave us haircuts, short and sloppy, *like little gladiators,* he would say afterward, studying his work.

Anyways, twenty, twenty, twenty, twenty, twenty, twenty. Easy because I'm so light. Easy because I am so used to it. Easier than running because I don't have to use my lungs or anything internal that's caked with all of the bullshit I've breathed, all the hatred and the exhaust.

Dr. Greg made me work in the kitchen as a dishwasher. He said, "Shut off your brain." He said monks do repetitive tasks as a form of meditation. He said, "Find God in the dishwater."

I did. Every meal I would wash everything with one of those big spray nozzles on a snaking metal hose, those steam-cleaning boxes, scrubbing with Brillo pads until my shoulders hurt, doing the dishes for the whole facility by myself. Usually they had two dishwashers, but Dr. Greg requested that it just be me, so that I wouldn't have the free time after dinner. I moved my hands in concentric circles, applying more and more pressure the farther out I got. I did this until it turned into my body's sole purpose, until I was like an autonomous machine, until I felt nothing but the immediate physical reality — hot water, hot metal, popping clusters of foam, hard Brillo — until even those sensations went away, and I truly disappeared from the scene, and I was not me, not a thought or a feeling, no memories that unfold and replay over time, no brain zaps, and no hatred, a simple machine with an extending appendage that applies pressure in circular movements. And it felt good, it felt so good, release from the bondage of the mind, my mind itself retreating.

I could deal with the groups — sitting in a circle and blubbering about our childhoods, about who we thought we were. I could deal with the dishes and waiting in line for rubber food and medication in paper cups — green beans that taste like nothing, sticky pills. I could deal with the one-on-one sessions with Dr. Greg and the arts and crafts and the twelve-step speakers they would bring in. I could deal with the stupid guided meditations and their hokey mysticism.

I could not deal with mandatory dancing. Not Richard Simmons and his shorts, his positivity. His overweight backup dancers, his shitty live-band covers of '70s songs. His spastic flailing.

"The time has come for a brand-new you!" Arms outstretched, back in, shaking his hands up and down with loose wrists: "Are you working hard?"—three steps forward, two steps back—"I hope so!"—shoulder roll—"We're workin' hard for you!"

One younger guy got out of the dancercising because he told his therapist that he was homophobic. That he was molested when he was a kid, and just the sight of Richard Simmons filled him with rage. They let him walk circles around this grassy area by the far fence while everyone else danced. I asked Dr. Greg if he could get me out of it, and he said no. He said, "You need to learn how to do things you don't want to do. You need to learn how to take direction." Part of the terms of my probation were anger management classes. He said, "We can count this toward your Anger Management."

Dr. Greg drew out a graph for me. He turned a piece of paper on its side and drew an arcing line like a wave across it, like one of those frequency charts from physics class that sinks and rises in equal parts. He drew a smiley face at the high point of one of the waves and said, "This is where someone feels good," and he drew a frowning face at the bottom part. "This is where they feel down." Then he drew a straight line through it, right in the middle. He said, "But this baseline, this is consistent; in the end, it all averages out to around here." He labeled this line *Euthymia*.

After this, he drew another wave, lower than the first, so that the high points almost touch the average line, but the lower points stretched farther down the page than I would have liked. He said, "This is you. This is your ideal mood graph." He drew an average line through it, too, about two inches lower than the other. He said, "Your baseline will always be lower, but you just have to get used to it. The stable waves are what's important. And after a time, you won't know the difference."

Those two inches between me and the world.

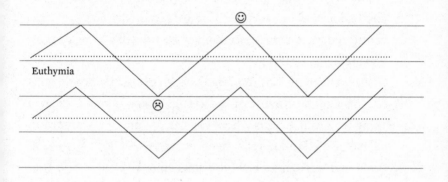

Euthymia

He got another piece of paper out. He turned it on its side and drew a much smaller version of the wave down the middle. "This is the euthymia line." He made a dotted line at the top, well over the crest of the wave, and wrote "hypomania," and another one way below the trough and wrote "major depression." He drew a crazy fucking line that swooped and dipped and squiggled across the page but mostly stayed down near the depression line. He said, "This is you unmedicated."

He said, "This dotted line is the mania threshold and this one is the major depression threshold." He pointed to the points rising up close to the mania line and said, "This is where you feel really good. This is where you engage in sexually risky behavior and start to undertake new projects or plans." And the one point that stretched higher than it. "This is where you disassociate — you start to have delusions, paranoia, grandeur," he said, "like when you told me you thought that you had access to every bit of information you had ever encountered, that it was stored in a library in your head, or that you are being followed."

He went to the bottom. The long, sweeping parabolic bottom that took up most of the graph. "Here is where everything feels dull; here is where you can't figure out if you want to live or die. And here" — he motioned to the lowest, lowest point and said, "here is where you can barely move, and you are sure that nothing will ever be better, that this is all there is, and you know you want to die."

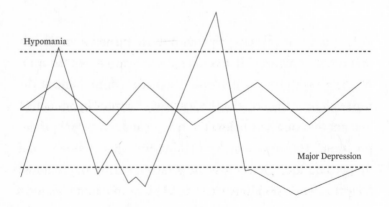

He put the pages in a folder and gave them to me. He told me that I should start keeping a graph of my moods. I liked the honesty and the tangibility of the charts. But there was no room on them for anger. Which was negative but exciting. Or that feeling of being completely submerged in the ocean at night — calm, almost depressing, but overwhelmingly warm and secure. If the x-axis is time, what is the y-axis? Had Dr. Greg found a way to quantify goodness? He wouldn't ever answer my questions directly, and I figured if he actually knew what he was talking about, he probably wouldn't have been working for the state, anyways, paid like shit in some fucked-up lockdown mental facility with a bunch of indigents and criminals in backwoods central Florida.

Sometime after I fell off the jungle gym, my oldest sister took my brother and me to the pool. He was with his friends again. She put me in the shallow end while they splashed around on the other side. They were dunking her and climbing all over her, just a mess of arms and legs and water erupting up into the air. I must have gotten distracted watching it because I had drifted to where my feet couldn't touch anymore. I went over to try to climb on her back too, but I got immediately thrown off. I was sinking and flailing and trying to keep my head above water to call out to my sister, to get her to notice me and put me back where I belonged. I bobbed like that for a while, getting lower and swallowing more water through my open mouth, trying to muster the breath to yell loud enough for her to hear me. I guess eventually she noticed, but I don't remember anything after that.

"Don't you think it's interesting that your brother is with his friends in these memories, but you are alone?" Dr. Greg asked.

"I guess."

"Do you think that you have been fighting for attention, drowning and yelling for someone to notice you, to help?" We had been in his office for about an hour, and I was starting to get really uncomfortable. I just wanted a cigarette.

"I don't know," I said.

"You wanted to have fun. You wanted to be with everyone else, splashing and laughing, but you ended up alone, feet off the ground, unable to join them, and unable to get back to safety. Stuck, treading water, and sinking. Does that sound familiar?" He was kind of smiling now, clearly pleased with himself.

"Yeah."

"Aren't drugs supposed to be fun?"

"They are fun," I said.

"Not for you. Not anymore."

"Yeah, not anymore."

I had never thought about any of this before. Dr. Greg had some points. He usually did. Framing my life in this way, building these narratives, had a certain allure. But it seemed reverse engineered, a trick you could learn like fortune-telling or horoscopes. This kind of cause and effect, the linear movement, explanations — they were paralyzing. They were sad. They went backwards with a writer's brain and added a bunch of shit in between the lines. They put me like a tiny actor on a gigantic stage, reading a script and waiting for the rest of the cast to show up and hand me a prop.

Later, I heard that humans actually got smart from social interaction, that tons of animals use tools and that primates were using them long before humans evolved, but what really fertilized our consciousness was having to interact and keep track of a bunch of different other humans, coordinate with them, not just socially but practically. That was how our brains really grew.

People prefer to live and interact within communities of about 150. That is the magic number. There are radiating circles and levels within this 150, closer and closer to the subject, 5 intimate friendships, 50 bonded relationships, but 150 is about the number our brains could handle and sort with meaning. This number had apparently grown over time. Our old tool-wielding ancestors from a million years ago could handle about 50 others, the next species 75, and on and on. Beyond the 150 you have acquaintances, and beyond that, faces that register as vaguely familiar, that are filed in your head somewhere as having been seen before, but you can't quite place where. Beyond that, I guess, just shapes: noses and eyes and skin, uncontextualized and strange.

I figured my community was smaller than 150. Much smaller. Maybe around 15 or 20 tops, but you could make a case for it really just being one. I was one of those old, unevolved guys, tapping stones together, trying to make do.

•   •   •

After the pool, my sister took everyone home. When she parked in front of our house to unload the car, she pointed to the grass and said, "Stay right there. Don't move." She sounded like she was mad, and I still felt like I was in trouble for what had happened at the pool. I stood where she pointed. After a few seconds, I felt something on my legs, and I realized I was standing on an anthill. There were hundreds of them crawling over my ankles and my calves, biting me. I called my sister's name, but she either ignored me or couldn't hear. I didn't want to move from my spot. I didn't want to disobey her again. I still get that allergic feeling, tingling unease by my ear and down my arm, when I think about it.

"That is why you have problems with authority," Dr. Greg told me.

"I love my sister."

"I believe you," he said.

"It's not like she wanted me to get bit by ants. She just wanted to make sure I didn't get hit by a car in the street."

"But she didn't hear you calling," he said.

"Besides, she's a girl. I only lose my shit when guys tell me what to do."

"How old was she?" he asked.

"I don't know. Like twenty."

"When you're just a boy, everyone is your father. Even your sister."

Later, I learned that Dr. Greg wasn't even actually a doctor. He was a social worker.

*   *   *

"Summer in the City," "These Boots Are Made for Walkin'," "Soul Man," "My Boyfriend's Back," "Respect," "I Will Survive," "Wipe Out," "Ain't No Mountain High Enough."

"It's sweatin' time!"

"And kick!"

"And roll."

"One more time!"

I couldn't take it. His voice bounced around the walls of my skull, getting louder and louder, scratching and scrambling everything. In the middle of "The Locomotion" on a Tuesday, we were sliding back and forth, making little mock-running gestures with our arms, and I walked out the door. They brought me in front of the director and Dr. Greg and a couple of the other therapists.

I sat at the end of a long table and told them I wasn't going to do it anymore. I said I would do anything else, just not that — refusing treatment, noncompliance. Dr. Greg said if it happened again, he would violate me. The judge had been clear: *successful completion of all phases of treatment.* I thought about Fernando heading back to county to wait for his sentence, court then prison. I wondered how long he got. The director looked at my file and said, "Is it really worth five years? Richard Simmons?"

I was sitting on Julian's bunk playing Uno. Me and him on the far sides of his cot like we were at a sleepover. He was just some kid like me. Nineteen or twenty and already a perennial fuckup. He stayed in the back of the group during Richard Simmons, too, but he was gradually moving forward, learning the moves and blending in. That night he said, "I don't know about you, but I'm not going to prison over some Richard Simmons bullshit."

He said, "This is the state we're talking about. The big, fat dick of the state. It's gonna fuck you no matter what. If you fight it, it just lasts longer and goes harder."

He hit me with a skip and then a +4.

"Do what they say. In ninety days, you can go to some half-way house and pretend like this shit never happened."

I drew my cards and knew he had a point. I knew it, but I didn't think I could do it. I could walk into the group room knowing it. I could walk in there with one single objective: do it. I could want to do it; I could need to do it, but that was no guarantee that I was going to.

"Uno," he said. "Just focus on that girl behind Richard with the fat ass — do the Locomotion with her, that's what I do."

Julian gave me an idea. I told Dr. Greg that I couldn't stop jacking off. I told him I couldn't sit still in group without obsessing about whoever, some girl I used to know or what-ever female tech was working that day. I hadn't so much as thought about sex in months, but I thought it would make him up my Risperdal on account of my history with mania. I was right.

He recommended that the psychiatrist put me on an extra two mg in the morning. I thought this would chill me out and help me obey the rules. I was right again. I felt like a genius for a little while, and then I felt like a zombie.

●   ●   ●

Dwight would do the floors while I did the dishes. I would talk to him, but mostly I listened while we got on with our chores. I learned that he'd requested to mop the floors. Even with his one leg, which I figured must have hurt or at least gotten uncomfortable from all that swaying while he rubbed the mop across the greasy tiles.

He would say, "Idle hands are the devil's workshop."

I felt good about adding Dwight to my radiating circle of people to keep track of. He was always succinct like that in his Bartow twang, his slow drawling voice like a southerner out of a movie. I always thought he looked like George Foreman but with hair. He was about as big, too. I told him this once, and he said he gets that a lot.

He said, "You know he's got twelve kids. Five sons and he named every single one of them George, can you imagine? Now that's an ego," he said. "I named my first son Dwight Jr., but that's it. His other brothers've got names of their own."

"But, shit," he went on, "could you imagine if when your daddy hit you, George Foreman hit you?"

Between Dwight and the dishes, I figured I was slowly evolving. Tools. Social interaction. He would tell me jailhouse stories from back in the day as he mopped. "I became a man in prison" — pause — "in the *eighties*." Like that meant something, and by the stories he told me, I guessed it did. Reagan, AIDS and rape and crack and the Nation of Islam and the skinheads. He was the type to share in every group we had, and when he did everyone would listen because he was such a good storyteller. He would go on and on for ten, fifteen minutes sometimes, stories that would maybe start off related to the topic but would ramble and twist around and end up somewhere completely different, sometimes ten, fifteen years away from where they started, and it would always leave a silence in the room afterward like that feeling of shuffling out of a movie theater after a real good matinee, where you forget it's daytime until the sun shrinks your eyes in the parking lot.

I always wanted to ask him about his leg, but I didn't want to be rude or nosy, and I thought that, too, was evidence of evolution. Eventually he just told me.

He said, "After I got out the second time, I was thirty-three. Like Jesus, thirty-three and ready to be nailed up to something somewhere. I don't know nothing or how to do nothing. I got a job with a landscaping crew. I was a high flyer, you know. Treetop man. You ever been to Lakeland?"

I had been to the county detox there once.

"Well, they got those big-ass tall trees in Lakeland. Fifty, sixty feet. Shit, sometimes eighty. Big bald cypress trees and longleaf pines. And I would get harnessed up and go chainsaw the branches way up top. Well, one day, after I had been working there almost a year, and, I kid you not, I had just started sliding back into my ways, *just* started. Maybe a week in. Started smoking and drinking again and all that, blowing my paychecks on slow horses and fast women, and I was up there one day, drunk as a skunk and fooling off, getting fancy with the saw, and I slipped and I hit my head on one of the branches so hard it cracked my helmet, and the ropes snapped tight and caught me before I went too far, but the saw swung around and got my leg. I woke up in the hospital and my mama was there staring at me, and you know what she said?"

"What?"

"She said 'Dwight . . . the Lord done slowed you down.' First words outta her mouth," he said, laughing.

I thought about my slippery hands on the metal rungs of the jungle gym. I thought about my mother and her dress and Dwight's mom and the big-ass tall trees in Lakeland, vomit, and chain saws. He and I were two early men looking for God in soapy water, trying to get a little more evolved in the cluttered silver kitchen and the cloudy settings of his mind.

On my new meds, I was trying to think whenever I could; I'd sneak in a few thoughts before the pills kicked in and slowed my blood down and turned me dumb, dry-mouthed, and hungry. I started to get really preoccupied with one idea: how do thoughts start?

They brought the head psychiatrist in to give us a lecture on the amygdala and the frontal lobe, about behavior regulation and the addictive problem. It all seemed so simple. Like they had it all figured out. He had more graphs. More diagrams. It made sense to me, and this guy had credentials. But I kept thinking: Okay, brain activity is little tiny chemical messengers shot electrically across synapses. Okay. These are the chemicals that regulate your mood, that make sure you breathe, that turn stimuli into sensory information, that cause pain and pleasure and motivate behavior and help you go to sleep on time, that control your muscles, everything.

Everything, I get it. But what about when there is nothing, and you are just sitting around, no sensory changes and your mind is just running, jumping from one thing to the next. Recalling and imagining pointless random shit. What if I could fly? What if I wasn't in this stupid place? How many times a day do you breathe? Remember that time when you were young and you saw a manatee while you were swimming at the mouth of the river, and you held your breath for two minutes following it? How long have manatees been around? Remember the barnacles growing on the manatee's back? What is a barnacle? An animal, some kind of underwater plant? Wouldn't it be nice to be a manatee or even a barnacle?

What exactly is all of that? Where did that come from? I get how the chemicals make you do things. But how the fuck do they get converted into language? Is it accidental or is there some part of me controlling it, beyond it? Pushing it around?

I was sure I could figure it out if they took me off my meds, so I decided to ask Dr. Greg.

"Why do you want to know that?" he asked. "Do you think it's because you are feeling powerless here, and you want to exercise your will over the situation in some small way?"

Dr. Greg, you bastard.

"I'm just curious. You don't have to turn everything into therapy, you know?"

"I'm your therapist," he said. "Nobody knows for sure. Does that bother you?"

"It bothers me that it doesn't bother you. I'm just a fucked-up kid. You're supposed to be the expert."

"You're not a kid, you're an adult. You're nineteen years old."

He told me to pray. And told me to write down a definition of the word "soul," what I thought it meant, and what I thought about it. He asked me to consider consciousness and the "I."

We weren't allowed to have books in there, that rule came from higher up the chain than Dr. Greg, but he wrote down the titles of some books to check out when I got out: *Meditations on First Philosophy, Republic, On the Soul.* He said maybe I should go to school when I got out, if I was stable. He said he could help me look at community colleges when I got closer to being released.

"I didn't graduate high school," I said.

He helped me schedule a time to take my GED test after I left treatment, but I didn't show up.

He pointed to the word "Republic" on the paper. "Plato wrote in dialogues. He thought the soul was made up of three parts: reason, spirit, and appetite. He uses the metaphor of a chariot with two horses. Do you know what a chariot is?"

I nodded.

"Well, one of the horses is tame and beautiful, the other wild and mean. They are meant to represent the positive and negative aspects of passion, of feeling and emotion. On the one hand, the nobility of spiritedness, the desire for recognition and respect from others, appropriate pride. On the other, appetites run amok. The charioteer is reason, tasked with guiding the whole soul toward harmony. But even the positive can lead you too far off track. The charioteer has to channel their energy together in order to achieve balance."

I thought about my medication. I thought about Richard Simmons directing the crowd.

"My chariot guy is asleep at the wheel," I said.

"Right now, the appetites are in charge," said Dr. Greg.

That night, before my Risperdal kicked in and chilled my brain into cold syrup, lying in my bunk in the open dorm, I thought about another early memory.

I was happy in this one — not distressed, not drowning, or falling, or being eaten alive. I was reading. I was in between my mom and my dad, and I had come to them on the couch to show them how I could read. I was holding a picture book, the one about the boy who gets sent to bed without any dinner and travels to a land where big magic animals have parties in the jungle. Only, I started reading it to them for the first few pages, and somewhere along the way I got bored. I started to stumble, and my brain wandered in and out, wanting to just look at the pictures instead of the words. So, I started to make things up, to just describe the images and imagine what I thought the words were saying. A picture of the boy on a boat with two lines of text next to it became an excited two-minute digression about the ocean, the jungle parties, the trees. In between my parents, feeling their warmth on either side of me. My mom was laughing, and my dad was smiling. They seemed genuinely impressed at my ability to go, to just pull stuff out of the air in between them, more impressed than when I read the words precisely, and so I went until I started to run out of energy, until I got tired on the couch and in my bunk, and the Risperdal kicked in and sent me to sleep smacking my lips, snoring like an idiot with everyone else in the dorm.

I finally graduated. Dr. Greg stood up on our last session and gave me a hug, which felt out of character for him, and he said good luck. Dwight was long gone, and I said bye to Julian. They gave me a black plastic trash bag and called a local guy from AA to give me a ride to the bus station. I didn't notice until I got in his car that there were lakes completely surrounding the little compound. Beautiful country lakes, smallmouth bass lakes. I had never seen the place from outside, either. I had only been in it. It was tiny, but the fence was expansive. It looked like an old elementary school, one story, mostly covered walkways leading from one tiny building to the next. I hadn't noticed, either, that the sign out front said TRI-COUNTY HUMAN SERVICES, which I thought was a funny name for the place but pretty accurate. Human services. Such a pleasant institutional name, like the Humane Society or the Department of Children and Families. I don't know where I had gotten the name Florida Center, I heard other people use it, even my public defender used it, and I could have sworn that's what it said on the piece of paper he gave me when I was in jail. The AA guy who gave me a ride to the bus stop was talking about something, probably AA. I twisted the top of the bag and looped it in on itself and threw it under the bus.

    I could smell the salt from the sea in the air as soon as I

stepped into the bus station downtown. It smelled like low tide and home. I borrowed someone's phone and called the number of the halfway house manager that Dr. Greg had given me. He said he would be there in twenty minutes, and I went across the street and bought a pack of 305s. I hadn't had a cigarette in months. It tasted like shit, this bus-stop 305. It tasted like the first cigarette I had ever smoked, and a small part of me regretted picking it up again. But I smoked another one, and another, and they started to taste better, and I got a nice head rush.

The halfway house was a couple of duplexes next to each other. The manager gave me a key, and I moved into my unit and got settled in that way I used to get settled. Carve out a little rat's nest corner of my own in a space that rotated ownership. I slid my little key in the lock and opened up the unit, sat down, and found myself and the room, all there ever seemed to be. It reminded me of the key my parents had given me to unlock the house when I got home from school when I was little. My first key, and how lonely a key is, because it means no one is home where you are going. No one is there to let you in, and after a lonely day of school, being put in one room or another, handed pieces of paper and given directions, walking around aimless and siloed amid the noise, I would get home and I would put the key in the lock myself, open the door myself, sit myself, make a sandwich from the fridge for myself. Lonely, everyone at work, my brother at some practice or another. My mom's loopy cursive handwriting all over the kitchen in schedules and address books and notes on the fridge, a letter from her hand on the counter, telling me about dinner, how to heat it up or whether I should wait — saying love and meaning it. And that's how the half-way house felt when I first walked in off the bus stop and how it would later feel when I'd get home from work, sweating and stinking like grass clippings, quiet and lonely, the unoccupied room so still. And just like I would do when I was a child, I would sneak around quietly, so as not to disturb the stillness of the room, to make it as close to how it was when I wasn't around. Sometimes, I would just sit down at the table and stare, do nothing until my mom got home, just be still like the room itself. From an empty room, any empty room, I can hear the life of my brain like a story told backwards.

9

I WAS LIKE A MOLE. I hadn't seen the sun, really, for a long time. Not the real sun, the August sun. I was pale, and I was soft, and I craved outside. So, the first chance I got, I rode the bus over the Intracoastal and went to the beach. It took me a while to get there, even though it was only a few miles away. I was still taking my medicine, so I was practically asleep on the bus. I got off and the place was teeming with tourists. It made my head hurt. There were families and couples and white noses; there were seagulls eating trash and making their boomerang calls, back and forth like taunting laughter. I stood by the fence around a condo pool and watched a heron stalk on the ledge, its long, crooked neck and legs, its sharp beak pointed toward the water, waiting hungrily for a fish to show up in the clear blue chlorine.

I sleepwalked over to the pier and saw a little kid with

a Coke can handline, the fishing line tied to the tab and wrapped around the red can. It was some kind of hood science; the kid couldn't have been more than eight, and he was sitting there with his legs over the pier and his chest against one of the wooden railing posts. His arms were wrapped around the post and holding the can out toward the water. I sat there watching him, hoping he would get a bite because I wanted to see him bring something in with that rig. Nothing happened, so I went out to the hot sand and the green water. I waded in and let the water kill my senses and salt my brain. I floated like bait, waiting for something to grab me, and it did, a memory of when I learned how to swim. When my dad took me out here in the ocean, the Gulf, rather. Salty and warm. I was four or five and kicking upright, violent kicks to keep myself from falling under, and he backed up away from me. *Swim to me,* he said. And I did, or I tried to. No instructions, no strokes, just *swim to me,* necessity the mother of invention, I had to invent swimming from scratch, as if I was the first person to ever venture out into the sea, flailing and propelling myself with sheer will. And just as I get to him, he backs away, and I am stuck in that moment, fear and suspension, my father farther than how he seemed, me searching for him, eyes open in the sudden flashes of water above and below, salt burning them, moving into my nose, down my throat. Forward, pushing myself forward, him, leisurely backing up, moving the bar, the way he made enrichment harder, just as I'd find it easy, he'd buy a higher-level book, just as he upped the number of push-ups I had to do as soon as I got a handle on them. Love and lesson in every backward step, more dis-

cipline shot deep into me, into the fibers of my muscles and
the strands of my DNA: *men are made,* not found, *like little
gladiators.*

I pulled myself out of the water, dripping wet from salty
memory. I laid the towel that I got from the halfway house lost
and found across the sand, and I promptly fell asleep in the
sun, feeling its intrusion into my skin. I dreamt of fish, of fishing, of grabbing squirming shrimp from the bait bucket and
hooking them through the back. Of childhood, my brother
and I riding our bikes out to the bay with our fishing poles
balanced on our handlebars. I dreamt of wading out into the
mangroves, our bikes lying in the mud. I dreamt of a snook I
hooked once, big with a mean black stripe down its side. It hit
my shrimp and took off, and once it figured it was hooked, it
swam back toward me, toward the dock, and it swam around
a pylon a few times, then darted away, cutting my line across
the barnacles at the water's edge. I woke up on the beach, and
the sun was lower, and my body was screaming in pain. I had
been asleep for six hours in my dumb Risperdal coma, and
I hadn't been in the sun in a year, and my chest was already
deep red. It was bubbling and itching, and the next day I was
covered in blisters and ultraviolet pain.

I got a fever and chills, and I shut myself in my room and
was so dehydrated and confused I thought I was gonna die. I
took some Tylenol along with my meds, a fat handful of pills,
and I could feel them move through my guts like a wad of
melted plastic, dissolving little by little and sliding into my
fever. I asked my roommate to buy me a can of Coke at the gas
station down the block. I couldn't understand how light had

done this to me. Even the light from the lamp burned my skin, and I was seeing spots. I turned off the lamp and sat in my room, smacking my dry lips, sticking to the sheets. The Coke, sweet and cold, put me in the dark and settled me. I was underwater, breathing through bubbles, and clouds of shrimp were swimming through the air, schools of minnows moving together feeling tickles in their lateral line systems. Snails were inching across my skin, their fat shells gently protruding, and my mouth was full of barnacles, fishy and stony and salty. Salt everywhere, burning in the corners of my eyes and in the deep caverns of my sinuses. I moved to the pitch-black bathroom and showered blindly in cold water, only it felt like a reverse shower, like the air was the water and the droplets from the showerhead were dry. I wrapped myself in my blanket and sweated and shivered. I was in an evil reef, sunken and still, and I was breathing through my blistered skin. In an underwater hell, tortured by the tides' violent swaying across sessile life, by scores of fish and cnidarian demons doing the retributive work of a vengeful sunken god. I am paying for the transgressions of a land-borne life, for a lifetime of motility and action — respiration, my original sin. And something within me knew that even when this broke, when the fever released me, it would never fully be gone, its beating would follow me above, and my chest would scar and metastasize, until a cancer could finally claim me, once and for all, back to the ocean floor, grab my ankles and pull me down to the submarine hell, where I would take my salty blows forever.

•   •   •

When I was thirteen, we had five hurricanes come in that season, and one of them was ripping up the Gulf Coast, skimming the shore, and moving toward Tampa from Naples, and as it spiraled up, the north winds were blowing so hard and sucking everything into the low pressure of the eye that the water in the bay all got drained out. My brother and I heard about this, and we rode our bikes over to where the river met the bay, and we climbed down, and we walked across all the newly exposed muck. Walked clear over to Davis Island, walking across the seafloor, stepping over dead fish and dying mollusks, smelling the salty rot of it all. And somewhere out there on the walk was a shock of green, a pasture, the seagrass that normally swayed and looked brown in the murky water was lying flat and shining green, greener than the grass on land, and dotted in the hidden meadow were some lone scallops drowning in the empty air, small and purple, covered in hairy algae. I picked one up and held it in my hand, and my brother said, *You know they can swim, right?* I held it up to eye level; it looked like nothing more than a little doomed button, pulsing and gasping like the sharks do when you catch them; it felt like nothing more than a rock. *They open and close their shells and float like butterflies through the water,* and he made a motion with his hand like a sock puppet, snapping the jaws shut and moving his arm backwards toward him.

And I thought, in my blistered fever, about the delicate line between things, the hazy, fragile boundary, not quite as distinct a definition as it seemed. This little rock that can swim. Half creature, half nothing. And if I closed my eyes and blocked my ears, I could recede into that hazy spot, where

I both am and am not, where I neither am nor am not. I thought, *What's so special about it, anyways* — being — why's it better than the other one. And I wanted to see, I wanted to strip all the matter away, hack it away like a coconut shell, and see what was underneath, to see if that animating flame of life in the center was worth all the hype, or whether it was still like a rock, wasn't life at all, just the same as the other. And just like everything else, the day after the hurricane, the tide shot back, farther than ever, flowing over the seawall and out into the city, right up over the road, and lapped at people's doorsteps. As everything that should have been underwater was exposed, everything that was supposed to be exposed was underwater.

Someone told me, in twenty years, thirty years, some number of years not so large as to be incomprehensible, Florida will end. The Atlantic and the Gulf will slowly draw closer to each other, taking their time and savoring each millimeter that brings them closer to their congress, reveling in the destruction of the distance that kept them separated for so long and everything that distance contained. In a few hundred years, they'll meet completely. A meeting full of predestination and longing, millennia in the making.

I imagine it slowly but sudden, like one day I step outside of a motel room and find a centimeter of water covering the ground. I don't think anything of it, I splash through the world up to my regular business, looking for money, and then months down the line, another centimeter. By the time I die, there's water up to my knees, the foundations of houses eroded by the constant lap of the tide, buildings slipping into the ocean, cars stuck stranded with salt eating at their tires and engines. Tampa gone back into swamp; the remaining structures sticking up in the shallow water like cypress knees, like the skeletal fingers of mangrove roots. Me, in the middle of the flood, soggy-footed in my sneakers, squatting on a mailbox smoking crack and watching the water wash away all evidence of my and everybody else's misdeeds.

I forget what's causing it: cars or litter or land development or toxic waste or what. The ozone or the polar ice caps or the deforestation or the glaciers. Some combination of these causes and interactions. But it jived with everything I knew about the world, because there is a fact about my life that has run parallel, alongside every memory and moment throughout the years. It is this: where I live is hot. Really fucking hot. Wet, stifling jungle heat. Sweat. On my forehead and under my arms. As a boy, sweat beading on my upper lip where, later, hair might be. Sweat on my feet and on my ass, by my balls. The loud and perpetual sun screaming from the sky like a fat, burning baby desperate for attention. Even where there are no palm trees, there is heat. In the shaded oaks that look more like Georgia than Florida, it is hot. To describe it any figurative way, with any words that correspond to real things in the world — an oven, a sauna — is to do it a disservice.

You say, "It's hot as fuck."

"It's hot as shit."

"It's hot as hell."

"Goddamn, it's fucking hot out."

And heat is exhausting. Heat can turn a nap into a marathon, and you wake up exhausted. You walk outside for a minute and you're sweating. The twenty-yard walk from the bus stop to the door and you're drenched.

And then you live outside — you don't have an inside and the heat becomes your great fact. You become permanently covered in a slick layer of oil and grime and sweat. I have heard about the homeless guys up north freezing to death in the winter — and, don't get me wrong, that sounds miserable, and cold is pain, acute and sharp — but heat, heat is constant and delirious and stifling. Throbbing and aching on those summer days, I would have loved to die frozen.

That's how I relearned to read, avoiding the bully sun, hiding in the dry cold public library downtown, sitting cross-legged on the ground reading Goethe or the *DSM*, back issues of the *Saturday Evening Post* or Emily Dickinson. I would move my finger letter to letter as I read sometimes or mouth the words if I was having trouble concentrating. I was educating myself in a strange and methodical American way. I was learning about urban Europe and New England, Christ and Freud and Horatio Alger. Julius Caesar, King David, and Antigone. I started with stuff I remembered from school or things people had told me about, and then a reference in one book would lead me to another, jumping through wormholes, but I couldn't understand what I was reading, and it would only lead me back in time, each book referring to books already written. And I couldn't tell you what the Top 40 looked like or what movies were up for the Oscars. I got mixtapes and bootlegs from my crack dealer, but I probably wouldn't have known if New York got nuked or if a pandemic swept the nation. I got current affairs fifth-hand through my meth dealer — doused, soaked, and prismed through amphetamine conspiracies and race hate. I was hanging by a sweaty finger off a panhandle on the underside of the big fat whale, ready to slip off and get lost in the Gulf or the Atlantic.

Like Dr. Greg said, it was Descartes that my brain liked to eat the most. Him and Plato sitting with me on the bus and in the woods, at the probation office and in the sweaty heat of the crack houses. Plato throwing his shadow puppets on the wall. Descartes bracketing off the entire world, suspending all belief and diving to the ocean floor, grabbing at the ground and bringing a handful of sand up to the surface, coming up with only himself and his thoughts there in his hand and in his head. I couldn't control it, but that was what stuck with me. I couldn't control it. I couldn't. Always starting with *I*. Always the subject, always the filter through which. *I* was the great assumption that I labored under, and I was getting so tangled up in the sensations and the needs. *I* was a knot that got further tangled the more I tried to loosen it. I was pushed and pulled, but I was doing the pushing and the pulling. The crack and the meth, they were just manifestations of myself, they were the bits of my wishes, pure and uncut self, inhaled and injected back into myself. I could tell that Descartes eventually got to a belief in the world from his post of skepticism, but I couldn't get there. I couldn't see it. I couldn't follow, and I was eating myself. I was so hungry that my stomach was consuming itself, but even that was an illusion — I had never seen my stomach, I had only conceived of it. I was coming apart at the seams. I was locked in the theater watching the play of my mind onstage, watching the information come in and out and dance across the lobes. And I was stuck in the theater screaming, "Don't go in there!" but I was, all the while, controlling my hands and my feet, moving them in there.

In the room, the library full of people, it was like whatever book I read was trying to erase me from it, trying to erase itself, my eyes passing over each word like an eraser and imbibing only the ideas they contain. But that is just how it seems, that isn't how it is. The room is the room, and it exists, and the librarian watches me the way she does every day with a mixture of hate and pity. And the shelves are endless and made up of the spines of books dyed in so many colors that at a glance they all seem gray. And the room fights back against the book, too. The world will not let itself be forgotten, each tick from the clock on the wall, each rustle of pages and click of the mouse, each beam of light through the window or showering down from the plates in the ceiling, all of these things pull me from my thoughts, from the words that try to destroy them. Even the book fights back, its texture and its position, the pages sticking together or a mark in the margins, a dog ear, these things fight the disappearing words. The words themselves fight back, their physicality, their font and length, their spacing, they distract me, too, break my concentration until I am left wondering what is what, what is trying to erase the inky letters, what is left after the letters are erased. I look to the clock, but the right half is blocked by a bookshelf and the exposed half is empty of everything but numbers, so all the hands must be in the east, in the lows, all lost behind the bookshelf, so I had no way to verify their existence really.

Roasting my brain at high temperatures, microwaves, and everything that went in wouldn't come out, but it wouldn't get organized on the horizon of meaning, either. It just floated around getting zapped, fried, and charred — the education unmoored from time and context, allowed to drift down lines of thinking that were just plain wrong, nonfactual, with no teacher to correct my course. But my head was getting filled; sometimes it felt just about full. I was starting to wonder if it would run out of room, how big it was in there, and I would close my eyes and try to imagine what the inside of my brain looked like, and I would see outer space. I would see a block of Aquinas floating like a planet with a few moons of James Joyce rotating around it, and farther out, Augustine with a Melville moon and all of this revolving around a boiling sun of fiery Plato, swirling along with everything else in a big galaxy of words and shit I couldn't be sure if I understood, organized around a center I couldn't see. And then my leg would itch or I would sneeze or get a stomach cramp and open my eyes for a second and try to go back, but everything would be out of whack, no magnetic field, no pull, no connection, just random floating like an old screensaver, and I would know I was full of shit; that is to say, it was empty, there was more room than I knew what to do with, it was hollow and the shit I was cramming in barely took up any room at all, in fact, it just got smaller the further in it got, more compressed, and the little ball of knowledge floating around like the screen-saver icon stayed the same size no matter what I tacked onto it. I'd rub the dirty library carpet with my open sweaty palm and look at some crusty dude jacking off on one of the computers, and I'd wonder what he saw when he looked at the inside of his brain. I would wonder if his head was full of that mixed-up garbage, too, and if he was jerking off in the library so he wouldn't have to look at it anymore.

And I kept coming back to Descartes, with his rigid two-substance system — the mind and the body — separate, distinct, made up wholly of different fabrics. Fundamentally unalike. One here, in time and space, and one outside of it, in a different realm, reaching down and, in a way I never quite understood, interacting with the other, pushing its buttons, manipulating it from far out in the ether. I went to the bathroom, shot up, and put my hands on either wall of the stall to steady myself while my eyes and ears shook. At the end of his book, there were letters back and forth between him and some princess. She was pressing him on this interaction, that much I understood, how can something immaterial affect something material? What would be the mode of their interaction? I couldn't understand his response, but I know he thought it happened in the pineal gland, some tiny little beating sac in the dead center of the brain. I checked out the Descartes book, so I could take it out onto the street and read while I smoked, but every time I took it out, the sun would blast my eyes, and when I came back in, the aftereffects of the light made the pages look pink and the words look green, and my stomach would start to tremble. It made me think of something someone at an AA meeting told me once as he handed me a copy of the Big Book. *In a book, there's two parts: the white part and the black part. Read the black part.* I thought that the black part is like the mind and the white part is like the brain. It's just a vessel for the other thing, the nonmaterial thing, to express itself. The black part, the physical instantiation of the words, isn't the mind itself but is just an effect of the mind. It doesn't contain all the vaporous possibilities of immateriality, but just one single expression according to its whims, and released into space over time. I knew that Descartes invented the geometric plane I learned in school. The *xy* plane, space governed by algebraic equations. Slopes on a grid. More instructions. And so, the pineal gland, I thought, is like a book. It's the blend. Where the two things meet, the ring in which the mind and body wrestle one another, push each other around. And so, I went to the reference section, to the medical encyclopedias with their drawings, and I looked for the pineal gland, that little ball of hormones that leaks my instructions into my brain. I knew Descartes was old, with an archaic understanding of medicine and anatomy; I wanted to see what really happened there. What I learned is that the pineal gland moderates my circadian rhythm, my sleep schedule, my internal clock. It drips melatonin and tells me whether it's night or day, winter or summer. It's where the sun places the hex of time on me, where it dictates my patterns, tells me whether to be conscious or not. And this threw me. Just when I thought I had a handle on it, on the dualism, now I had just the one thing, physicality. The same thing I always had: a sun and its children. It snapped me back, snapped my mind back, aware now again of the tininess of the ball bouncing slowly in my brain, the ball that can't grow and just drifts incompetently like the screensaver icon, just something to look at during dormancy. And so, I put it all down and went back to fiction. Or at least books that admitted they were fiction.

In between the creaking hard covers, I found passages I lingered on because they seemed so far away and strange. If they were fertile enough, I could forget who I was for a moment. I ran to omniscience. I hid in the plots and the lives, the many folds and nooks of a huge and sweeping map of humanity. I got lost with a turtle crossing a road in some square state I'd never been to, crossing slow and purposefully, getting hit by a car, dragging seeds through some decade past. I sought boredom. I liked to read pages where nothing happened, big long stretches of narrative diversion, the words just sounds in my head like a lullaby. The turtle crosses the road. The seeds are in his shell. I am nowhere. But then, then, in the next chapter I am there. In the bleached fields of dried crops that blow away. In the red and burnt faces of a sad family, slaving under the master sun. And after a while, I would read myself into anywhere. Hiding feverish with a murderer in St. Petersburg or lancing giants with a knight-errant, doomed on the high seas, in a loveless triangle in Paris. Everywhere I hid I was hunted and found by my own self, the ever-stubborn bloodhounds of my brain tracked me to all places, all these places I had never actually been. And so I caved. I gave up on reading; I allowed myself to be cuffed and brought back into the theater, strapped to the chair. And I eventually put the books away and moved to the sleeping computer bouncing its screensaver side to side, top to bottom. I shook the mouse and woke it and took my rightful place at the seat next to the man. To the hard slapping of porn into which I let myself slip, to occupy the vapors in the scene and insert my consciousness into the characters, the shadow people fucking on the wall, both of them me and both alive.

10

HOME AT 10 P.M. Hard for a little and then it isn't, just like everything else. Piss in a cup. Get some forms signed. Community service. Get a job. Therapy. Self-help groups. Go to Amscot, fill out a money order, get a Tootsie Roll from the bowl on the counter.

Hurry up and wait.

I had moved back from Palm Beach, so I had to switch POs, and I had to get serious. Rosario was my supervising officer down there; she let me call her by her first name. But up here was McKay, Officer McKay, and when I would go downtown to meet him — in that office building that was like a little slice of jail away from jail, in the waiting room, crowded and monitored — I would have to put on my hard face, cross my arms, and look ahead but look at nothing, not make eye contact but not avoid it. It was always a bit of a shock, coming in from whatever I was doing and being reminded that they could jump out and get me if they wanted. The AC cranked down low, the people behind the glass, everyone wriggling in their chairs. When I would go there, I would try to sit still and just fill out my forms with those tiny little golf pencils, but I always felt like, just for an hour, I was being reminded of something, and that, in a way, they wanted me to carry this little, cold, fluorescent-lit waiting room with me out into the world. Don't forget. Don't forget you are due back here.

The first time I met him, we went back into his cubicle, and he looked at all my papers, and he told me I hadn't done anything. He said, "I don't know how they do things down there, but up here you have to actually comply with the terms of your probation or you get violated."

Truth was I had just skittered in off a bender in north Broward. A horrific run that hollowed me out and might have fractured my brain for good. Rosario didn't check on me, but I knew I had to do something. The sober living house kicked me out, but they didn't rat on me. I got some sleep and some ice cream, and I took a bottle of niacin and drank three gallons of water. I sweated and pissed and purged everything out, got red and blotchy and scratched my skin off, and I came back to Tampa. I lied to Rosario and told her I had a job lined up. She didn't care; she was probably just happy to have one less person on her caseload. But I got into another halfway house, and I got in on a landscaping crew with one of the guys there.

McKay said, "You haven't done any community service. You're behind on your fees. It says you were signed up to take your GED in June—do you have your results yet?"

I shook my head. "I didn't make it."

He glared at me and scratched his pencil across the paper. "Let's start with the community service. But you need to sign up for a time to take your equivalency test before your next appointment."

He took me to the bathroom to piss test me, and I was sweating. The place was a fun house, mirrors above the urinals reaching all the way to the ceiling, and as I was trying to pee into the cup, I saw the reflection of his dark eyes staring at my dick. He looked up for a second and we made eye contact. "Some people use those fake dicks with clean piss to pass these things," he said.

I thought about squatting and coughing naked in booking, one officer in front and one standing behind you, standing open and cold and exposed, unwashed and still high, about to come rocketing back into yourself, into withdrawals, into jail. No nothing to ease the transition. I looked at the clean tile on the wall; I couldn't go. I was worried about the niacin, whether it had flushed me out good enough, and I thought about when I was sixteen and the seizure smashed my skull on the ground. Sitting in the hospital with a bandage on my head, wobbling to the bathroom with my IV to try to pee, my parents standing there at the foot of the bed in silence, until that nurse came in and grabbed my dick upright in his hand and shoved a catheter down into it. I felt that deep invasion in my pelvis still, that hand tight around my dick, standing there looking into the mirror, I felt the stiff needle push into my bladder. I thought about Walter, his naked, bloodless body. I thought about Bruce and his friends, full of blood. I thought

about the flaccid lifeless bodies of all the institution show-
ers and intakes and hospitals, weigh-ins, mass nudity, and I
thought about Mister, and I pushed to try to pee, but nothing
was happening except for the sweat building on my forehead.

McKay leaned over and turned the knob on the faucet.

I breathed deep and slow and it finally came, clean, and the
sweat on my forehead began to evaporate.

I'd wake up at five and get a ride with the guy from my halfway house. We'd show up to some yard across town and run
our Weedwackers right up against the curb, cutting perfect straight lines. We'd haul squares of sod or remove giant
branches, drag them noisily across the pavement; we'd run
our loud machines all day, the sounds of battle across the
quiet residential streets, battle against the forces of growth. I
was always shocked at how much the lawns grew. We would
go to a house, tame everything, beat their tiny little jungle
into submission, and then, in a week or two, come back and
find it wild again. I couldn't understand what made these
people, the homeowners, hate plants so much. At one house,
they had a brick driveway, and I had to inspect every little
space around the bricks, looking for tiny plants growing
through, "weeds," those plants that drove my boss nuts, that
drove the homeowners nuts. Unsanctioned life. But it always
came back, willed itself through the cracks and the seams
of the stones, and I knew it would come back, long after I
stopped coming, after the electric tools I used were all rusted
and eaten in a landfill, after me and the owners and the land-
scapers were all dead.

In the hot afternoons of those days, I could see my own nose, faintly down in the middle of my sight, or, if I closed one eye, it would form the edge of my sight, sweaty and hazy. It reminded me that I was behind it, always behind it, locked into a face I couldn't see, save for the fuzzy line of its one jutting feature, a killer's nose, and I was always crossing my eyes to inspect the lawn, my killing work, to see if it looked the way it was supposed to. If I looked at it normal, in focus, I could see each individual blade and leaf too closely, everything would look wrong, too seen, so I would take a few steps back and cross my eyes, try to take it all in the way someone who wasn't particularly looking would take it in. And all this wonky vision, combined with the herniating effort of my tenuous sobriety and the fuzzy mundanity of probation, turned me into an expiring clock.

McKay gave me a list of places that allowed violent felons to do community service. I looked it over and chose the American Legion. I helped the old guy there hang flags and change light bulbs. I would vacuum and set up chairs and tables for weddings or funerals or spaghetti dinners.

He would send me out to the veterans' cemetery and the parking lot to pick up the cigarette butts and dime bags and trash that would wash in with the rain. Hundreds and hundreds of plain white tombstones like little teeth sticking two feet out of the ground, six inches thick and three feet between them. I wouldn't even bother wearing gloves, I didn't care. I would walk around through the tombstones and the dead grass and look at the names and the dates and think about

Vietnam or Iraq or Afghanistan. I would wish I had joined the army and gotten yelled at and killed in some foreign desert and buried right here off Highway 60, where the summer storms could roll in and flood trash over my tombstone.

I never thought I would make it past twenty, which was where I was, and that sounds silly because it's so young, but it was, for those first three hard years, the closest thing I had to a milestone. I couldn't conceive of going past it. In those high teen years, I was young, and I knew it, but I didn't feel it. They felt like twilight years to me. Like the beginning of an end. I had heard, in the meetings and in treatment and out on the streets, a lot of people say they always figured they wouldn't make it past such and such an age. Usually it was thirty, but there was absolutely no way I could make it to thirty. Thirty was a number that I could not understand; it contained things like twenty-three, twenty-seven, twenty-nine — harsh, jagged, odd numbers. Just by the sound of them, I knew they weren't for me. Seventeen and nineteen were enough; they were jagged and hard enough for me to know that I didn't want anything to do with their older sisters. They had already killed me, more or less; left me in some waking purgatory, murdered the specifics of my life and turned me into a flat sieve, retaining nothing but gunk. But, I thought, it's a necessary delusion, this thing I told myself about not making it to such and such an age. Death, a bookmark, easier to place than living change, easier to understand than evolution, revolution. With death I can avoid the turn; it actually would be closer, less of a change from where I am. And if I died at twenty, it would be a kind of immortality.

This me would be the forever me, and I could not fathom any other me, so this was where I landed — soon dead — not as an arrival at any truth, but as a necessary idea born from my own lack of intelligence, existing as a cork to bottle up my own understanding. But in the field of the dead, in the graveyard, I understood that this was just wishful thinking, like those cults and religious sects that eagerly await the rapture, that worship it and welcome it, as a way of containing the here and now and having some frame with which to understand it, apart from the strangeness of the rest. Under my feet, the decayed and decaying bodies of the permanently young men, they are dead. Picking up the trash, I am, like it or not, alive. Those two things are different.

And throughout all that longing, another thought was cultivated, that there is another way that this ends, not with some foamy mouth overdose or suicide and hasty funeral, but a much more nondescript ending. McKay shows up to my house, I'm not there, I'm out howling into the wind shooting industrial chemicals into my veins, and he tests me the next time I see him, and I fail. He files a VOP, the judge sends me to prison, and I go rot. The years fuck my head irreversibly, and I get out and go back and get out and go back, and I turn fifty, alone, and one day one of those drug-addict diseases catches me — hepatitis, diabetes, kidney, liver failure, heart disease. The lining of my heart gets infected and inflated, my liver swells, my kidney shuts down, the speed fucks up my stomach so bad that acid burns holes into my gut and my throat, the wounds fester, ulcerous turns to cancerous, and I wither slow, unable to ingest anything, and one day, agonized

in a hospital bed, opiate tolerance through the roof, I die silently and slowly in an empty room, smacking that button,
that pain-management button.

I was starting to have these episodes. Brief and startling episodes of freezing. It felt like a gas bubble moving up my spine
and popping in my brain and just stopping everything for a
moment. Or like a power surge that would shut off the lights
and cause everything I saw to look radically different. They
would come and go in seconds and leave me shaking my head,
wondering what the fuck that could have been. I had been off
my medicine for a few weeks, and maybe that had something
to do with it, but it definitely didn't feel like it. It just felt like
one second I was seeing normal life in all of its movement and
meaning, and the next, everything was still, static and flat,
like a painting or a slide or a piece of paper had been put in
front of my face, a two-dimensional screen. Shadows would
become not evidence of depth or light but simply details on
the scene. Just something added to give the illusion of depth.
    And I knew these episodes were real because they took
time. Or something like it. I was lying on my bed in the halfway house, throwing a tennis ball up in the air and catching
it, which was something I liked to do because if I did it for
long enough it would put me into kind of a trance. I was sitting there never taking my eyes off of the ball, just watching
it rise, peak, and fall, rise, peak, and fall. And once I found
my rhythm, the sound it made when it hit my hand, the soft
but resonant *plop*, started to seem like a metronome. It made
the procedure seem regulated and stable, which I thought

was funny because it made the process seem totally backwards; it was like the sound was dictating the movement of the ball rather than the sound being a result of the ball hitting my hand. Once I did it for long enough, I couldn't remember what came first—the sound or the movement—and I couldn't remember what initial action had set the whole system in motion. Anyways, this was what I called meditation, but it was probably closer to self-hypnosis.

There was one light on in the far corner of the room, a dim old short lamp that looked exactly like a dim old short lamp. If you were asked to draw a lamp, this is almost surely what you would draw. And its light was weak, so the room had a soft, depressing yellowness to it. I started throwing the ball as the sun was out, and I didn't even realize the lamp was on because the room was so bright, but over time it had gotten dark and the lamp seemed to come on gradually. The window behind my bed faced west, so the sun went down behind my head. The foot of my bed faced the door, which was slightly open, and the door led to the kitchen, which was much brighter, so there was light coming in, but it wasn't enough to brighten the room. My roommate's bed was a few feet from mine on the opposite wall, and the old lamp was near the foot of his bed on top of a dresser.

I was lying on top of the covers of my bed with my shoes on and my legs crossed so that it looked like my right foot was where my left should be and vice versa, and I was tossing the ball. Rise, peak, and fall. My sneakers were gray, my pants black, the covers blue, the light yellow. When the door opened it swung toward my wall, and my roommate was standing in the middle of the light and he said, "Did you eat my Cap'n Crunch?"

And I caught the ball, and everything turned 2-D. The light from the door reaches the little lamp, and so the back is bright, my feet, my pants, and the covers are dark and shadowed, my hands are now on top of one another on my stomach with the neon tennis ball underneath them. I can see my whole elongated body and him standing at the foot of it, small and inquisitive. Everything is flat — he is on the same plane as the lamp and my feet. The door and the light flattened to right in front of my nose. I stare, not particularly at him but at the scene, I notice the edges of it, of the screen, but I can't perceive a world in which there is depth, in which there is an unseen room behind him and an outside world behind that. This is the all-encompassing picture in my face. And I stare, unfocused, at the collection of images and objects arranged along the x- and y-axes, the lamp is hovering somewhere in the middle of the room, weightless and unreal, sitting by coincidence on a dresser. My mouth is probably open.

"Yo," he said, "did you eat my fuckin' Cap'n Crunch?"

And I snapped out of it, and I said, "Nah, I just had a bowl."

"Don't do that, man. That's mine," he said, and he disappeared and closed the door behind him.

The room is yellow again, and I start to throw the ball a bit more, but I can't find the groove, so I go and take a shower and look at my hands. I hold up one hand in the falling drops of water, and I wave my other one underneath it to make sure that there is space between it and the floor. I feel the smooth corner between the wall and the floor to make sure that they are traveling in different directions. I close my eyes for a little and just try to feel the third dimension, to feel the depth that my body occupies, and I am sweating in between the streaks of shower water. When I get out, I make a note of the date on a piece of paper. I try to guess what the date was the last time this happened, and I decide that if it starts to happen more than once every two weeks, then I will try to get back on my medication. I label the note "Painting Calendar," so that it doesn't seem weird.

When I got to the auditorium, I was nervous. It was Halloween, and my leg was bouncing, and I was rubbing my hand on the coarse denim on my thigh. Some of the people taking the test were wearing light costumes, cat ears or makeup or cheap Party City nylon. All of us trying to skip out or long since skipped out on high school for various reasons. I had to shift over and scrunch to the side, so I wouldn't bump the girl next to me with my left elbow as I wrote. She was wearing a black tutu and had a witch's hat underneath her chair. Just the thought of the fabric bunching up under her was making me uncomfortable. I was shifting around, and I was worried that her skirt was going to fuck up my whole concentration. That all the time I would be jostling around, feeling the mounds of cheap nylon under my leg. She was still, she didn't even notice the costume, but throughout the first section that was the only thing I thought about: tutus, bunched fabric, crinkled noise. In the second section, I sat on my right hand and that helped. By the third, I didn't know where I was.

I always did well on standardized tests, for as long as I

could remember: the ERBs in elementary school, the SAT later, the ACT. I even took some subject tests: physics, English. I was good at it, and it was one of the only aspects of school that I actually liked. There was something between me and actual school, my inability to sit still and listen, to be open-minded, part of a class. The longevity of it was too hard for me, the whole year, I just couldn't do it. But for four hours, I could go. I could succeed, and I could tell I was succeeding as I was going, which was a rare and beautiful feeling for me, like the dishes, to just be in the zone, doing as I was told, making progress, not a thought toward anything else. I even liked the personality tests and psychological exams that shrinks would give me — the Minnesota Multiphasic Personality Inventory, the Myers-Briggs — simple call-and-response, question-and-answer.

I had a counselor in school talk to me once about the development of the prefrontal cortex in young men. He said we matured later, and that is why I was impulsive, why I had a hard time in class, my aggression, my lack of planning and social skills, my trouble with emotional regulation. He was the good cop, talking to me before some kind of suspension or something, some sort of trouble. This, the pattern of my life — me fucking up, getting punished, and then someone coming in and explaining to me why I behaved the way I behaved — Dr. Greg and Plato's chariot, my three earliest memories, the psychiatrist and my lizard limbic system, the guidance counselor and my frontal lobe, genetic predispositions — the situation of my life, whatever it was. Narrative was so important to these people. I guess it was important to me, too, in a different way. All of their ideas and stories relied on me having no agency whatsoever. They needed that. And however true it sounded to me, I needed some kind of agency. I craved it. I just wanted some reason that didn't lead to the dead end of predestination that haunted me everywhere I went.

Anyways, that's what I wrote about for the essay question. The topic was: *Is the current high school system sufficient to educate our country's youth? Describe what is valuable about our country's system or what might be changed in order to produce better results.* I guess I got a little off track. And I didn't do as well on the writing section. I never did. My math and verbal scores, always high, the writing, always lower. They gave me too much rope. I went all over the place, and I just got mad at the question, at the test. I got so distracted by hating the whole entire premise that I couldn't help but write muddled and circular nonsense. When I imagine someone grading my essay, I get mad. I imagine them looking for ideas, for mature sensible thought where everything is put in perspective. As if they themselves, the graders, don't feel that intoxication of confusion, as if there is no value in it.

After my dad had taught me how to swim his way — the terror of the ocean and the doggy paddle born from that — my mom would take me to the pool. She taught me the backstroke. She showed me how to float and then how to rotate my arms and kick straight at the same time. I was faster this way than the other, arms straight and perfectly circular in the air, my ears in the silent water, the clamor of the grounded world muffled and unimportant, and as the water dulled my other senses, washed them out, my vision became superhuman, and I could see the sky above me out of context, upside down and bright, crooked and new, and it was beautiful to see it this way. I was hypnotized by its inability to show me anything beyond itself—it looked like both the beginning and the end, exposed them as the same thing, the beautiful limit of the world. It propels me forward through the lap straight and fast, trying to get to the end of the sky, to see the other side of it, and it propels me headfirst straight into the concrete wall of the pool, that sudden blast of head trauma that breaks my spell and sends me back to the water and my mother, worried, wrapping me in a towel and looking through my hair at the knot rapidly growing on my skull.

And that was how I moved through essays, backwards, backstroke through time and knowledge staring at whatever there was until the wall came out of nowhere and put me back in place.

But Dr. Greg told me once that I needed to learn to be a "student of life." To listen to the various teachers in the world. A student among students, a worker among workers, learning and growing and doing. He said I walked around like I was an expert, but deep down I knew I wasn't. That this caused all sorts of rifts and problems with my worldview, that it kept me stuck and inactive. And I saw truth in that, too. So, before the test I did something completely foreign to me—I studied. I did a few practice math and reading tests, but I really tried to focus on the essay questions. They were so hard. It felt like they were specifically, tailor-written to everyone who had exactly what I lacked. I went to the library and found as many prompts as I could in a GED practice book.

1) Consider how our society has changed over time. Are young people today better off than they were in the past? Write an essay explaining why or why not.

2) If you won the lottery today, what aspects of your life would you change? What would you keep the same? Write an essay discussing your ideas.

3) If you could live in another time period, when would it be and why? Be sure to include relevant historical details.

I did all of them until I ran out. In my utter failure to think about the essay in the right way, I discovered some things about myself, things that I felt like the therapists and teachers and whoever else missed. (A) That I was actually pretty dumb. (B) That dumbness could be a kind of stubbornness, and it was self-centered and got more intense with time. I would double down on my dumbness and feed it back into itself, until I had a closed solipsistic loop, refining the details of a stupid idea, one that was spoiled from conception. And that's why my essays were nonsensical, impossible to access from outside my own loop. I would think they were good as I was writing them, and then, when presented with the information again, would find that my answers made no sense.

I would probably answer the questions a different way each time. And I could tell I wasn't getting any better, so I came up with my own prompts.

1) Who was the first person to turn a wolf into a dog? A forest into a park? Write an essay explaining the difference between these two processes.

2) Imagine you have no scientific or anatomical understanding. How would you conceive of illness? Of acute pain?

I think the first person to turn a wolf into a dog was the first person to feed it regularly. To turn a forest into a park, however, you just have to put a fence around it. The difference comes in what happens when you let go. If you remove the fence from a park, it will expand and grow outward; it will thrive. If you take away a dog's food and shelter, will he be able to find it on his own? Will he prowl the world like a wolf or die like a pet? I think the main difference is that turning a wolf into a dog fundamentally changes its physical character, whereas a park and a forest does not; it is just a naming issue.

I think I could understand pain pretty well because of cause and effect: I get hit, it hurts. This association is pretty well ingrained, and even with a modern understanding of "anatomy," this is still basically all I know for sure about pain. Sickness, I think, is more difficult. I had a friend once who would complain about his kidneys being dry. He would get some type of sensation in his lower back that made him feel like there was no fluid back there, which I thought was impossible and dumb, but he would swear that is what was going on. So, what I am trying to say is that even knowing your organs or knowing about the way bacteria and viruses spread just gives you more specific ways to make stuff up. It just hems in your imagination, and then gives you a more forceful belief in it. If he didn't know what a kidney was, he probably could have been convinced it was anything. I think fevers would trip me out the most, cold and hot, there would be no way to make sense of it. I would probably think it was some kind of ghost or evil spirit trying to take over my body. I don't know for sure, but I can practically guarantee that's what people thought back in the day. And they weren't far off, I guess. And back then, you might have gotten killed by a fever, or killed by some disease that caused the fever, and so I think it would have really seemed like some kind of supernatural stuff, your body being snatched into hell, kidnapped by the heat.

I finished the test early, and I ran out into the hot autumn wind and went back to my bed in the halfway house, and I replayed the questions in my head. Thinking of the ones that I knew I missed and what I might have missed about them. Trying to calculate my score. The essay, of course, incalculable.

On Monday, I told McKay. He said congratulations. He said I should celebrate whether I passed or not. So I took my roommate to an Outback, and we had a Bloomin' Onion and watched half a *Monday Night Football* game. I dropped him back off and drove to the bay, parked, and looked out over to the twinkling houses on the other side of the water, and the power plant farther out from that, and the giant, tan mountains of dirt from the phosphate mines in the hazy distance in the east. I remember once, when I was really little, mistaking the tiny bay for the yawning ocean, misjudging the abilities of my own sight against the undefeated power of distance, I asked my dad if those sandy pyramids were Egypt, and he and my brother laughed, and he said, *Maybe*. And he put his hand above his eyes like a sailor in a movie and he said, *We can't know for certain.*

11

I AM ON MY KNEES, and I am pouring sweat. It is a hot pregnant night, eighty-five degrees and wet with the collective sleep of the world. I am on my knees, and there is no ventilation, just my desperation radiating off of my sweaty back and hitting the little tin walls, bouncing back to me with greater and greater force. I am looking for little pieces of crack that I might have dropped on the dirty floor. I am pawing at the ground with one hand and holding my lighter with the other. Holding it close and putting my eyes to the dirt, getting so close that the flame singes a part of my eyebrow, holding it until it gets so hot that it burns my thumb, and I toss it, and I comb the ground with both hands. It is hot, and I wait for morning.

I had gone to find Bruce, shadow seeks shadow, to find his penthouse apartment, to find his poetry and his secure madness. He had a place. He lived somewhere fixed, somewhere he could go to perform his craziness. Not like me, always somewhere new and blurry, out in the open and calling attention to myself. He was in a locked room, and the only people who could bother him were people he wanted to bother him. So, I went to see if maybe he wanted me to bother him. I needed what a room provided.

His old number was disconnected, but I remembered him trying to track me down in AA to make amends to me. I got his new number off a list on the wall of an AA clubhouse and borrowed a phone to call him. He had bought a gentrifier bungalow in an up-and-coming part of town; he moved out of that penthouse, and he got clean while I was in jail. He told me I couldn't stay with him. He was doing yoga and eating paleo and some other shit — detoxifying — he was chairing the 5:45 AA meeting and ordering tea at the independent coffee shops sprouting up in his new neighborhood. He was off of everything except for the Klonopin for anxiety, but he said he was even weaning off that, too. I found a porta potty down the street at a construction site and banged a half a gram of blow and went and begged him for forty-five minutes and finally convinced him to let me hang out on the porch from ten until eleven every night in case McKay dropped by. He said he would let me use this as my address for probation, but I couldn't stay there.

I didn't have any missed calls from McKay, so I was in the clear.

Bruce said, "If I so much as see any of that shit, I'm telling your PO."

*   *   *

In the deep night, I broke into his shed to use it as a base. There was a little window by the alley, and he never went in there. The front door was padlocked, but when he was at work, I shattered the back window with my elbow and used my shirt around my hand to clean up the glass as best I could. He had a brand-new lawn mower, a Weedwacker, and a bunch of power tools. All of these things untouched; he hired a landscaping crew that came on Wednesday mornings. I think he bought them just to feel normal.

I am on my knees, and I am pouring sweat. It's dripping off the tip of my nose, and in that nanosecond between it leaving my skin and it hitting the ground, I forget what it is. And when I catch its movement with my dilated eyes in the dark, I think it's the glitter of a forgotten rock, and run my fingers over the spot where it fell, gently I slide my fingers across the ground to feel for any little fleck, but it's only a tiny circle of wet dirt. I repeat this movement over and over for hours. Each time forgetting the bead of sweat the second it leaves my skin, only catching that little flash of crystal movement, like a lure, like an injured minnow.

I stick my head out of the broken window and drink up some of that sweet alley air.

McKay came by and met Bruce, checked out the little house with hardwood floors and nice furniture, meticulously decorated with Bruce's new personality — Eastern religion and candles and yoga mats and books and cute vintage. McKay was impressed. I was gibbering like an idiot. Gritting my teeth to not talk so much. I started to say something about how Bruce's old penthouse looked, with the straight lines and solid colors—modern glass, marble, granite, but I stopped myself midway. After McKay was gone, Bruce tried to talk me into going to the Salvation Army, and I dove out into the night.

I no-called, no-showed for the second day in a row and my job was gone. I never went back. I never picked up any of the phone calls I missed from my boss, I just disappeared, let myself get swallowed by the immediacy of a broken brain.

The auditory hallucinations start. Not voices or anything, but a couple degrees away from voices. You think maybe you heard someone say something, far away, maybe from another world.

"What?"

"Did you say something?"

"Who's there?"

To the point where you can't keep still. You are looking around to see if someone is saying something. Or it sounds like you heard some feet shuffling up behind you, a cleared throat, a dog barking, someone crying, a made-up song that exists only in the silly recesses of your mushy brain.

In the small, hot shed in the early morning, penned in by the four simple tin walls, I hear a bird making a call like a child's toy from the trees, like a plastic laser gun flashing red beams into the dark, into my head, and the visual hallucinations start. Not full-blown yet, either, but shadow figures that intrude into the corners of my eyes, that shoot out from beyond my sight, the little shapes and people made of the imperceptible black stuff that surrounds my vision. It's this stuff, this goo just beyond the periphery, that never lets me settle down, that keeps me scared every second.

In the afternoon, I wait around the corner from the halfway house. I wait for the mailman. When he leaves, I go look for my last paycheck, but it isn't there.

I still have some money, but it's flying away from me, getting absorbed by the world at an unsustainable rate. I know this, and I decide in my horrific quickness to switch to meth. Cheaper and longer lasting. Crack is breaking me. For a moment, this seems like the solution to end all solutions. The greatest idea I have ever come up with. My problems are over.

At the Dollar General, I pace the drab aisles like a maniac. Turning around every ten feet to see if I heard that correctly.

"What?"

No one is there. I take two long, skinny candles and stick them in my pants, use the waistband to hold them up, and I walk straight-legged out the door to try not to crack them. I walk straight-legged to the bus and ride out east down MLK past one county jail, past the fairgrounds, and almost to another. I buy some ice in a raised trailer out there miles from the water, in the thick Spanish oaks and scrub palmetto, and I listen to the guy there tell me about chemtrails. He is coming apart, too — glassy blue eyes, glassy blue teeth migrating away from each other and rotting individually like trees in a forest eaten by beetles. He has a tight and narrow murderer's face. He has porn playing constantly on his tiny TV, and he says that jets are releasing barium into the air, that it gets into your brain through your lungs and makes you susceptible to radio-wave signals that can alter your emotions to such a precise level that they could make you angry enough to kill or calm enough to die. With a turn on a knob they could make you so horny that you could eat another person whole and not even remember it. And as he is talking, he meets my eyes and, beyond his voice, I hear his other voice, deeper and louder, somehow behind his audible words, and coming out of his eyes as they stare into mine, he says, *Hello.*

But with his larynx, he is still talking fast, and saying that the controls actually aren't 100 percent effective in everyone, but they spam different geographic areas at different times and can achieve about 20 percent effect, which is enough, and among that 20 percent they can pinpoint emotionality in a little less than half.

And he says, "Haven't you felt it? That whirring in the air that takes you over, gentle-like?"

And I have. The air like hot wires without resistance, deadly levels of current felt beyond traditional senses. I want to leave, but I feel like I can't, I feel the radio waves like he told me, and I feel the current of my blood so electric and paralyzing.

And he asks me, "Haven't you noticed how many people get killed around here in June?"

"That's how they keep us in check," he says, "keep us scared to go outside, scared of each other."

He sits down close to me on the couch and looks at the porn on the TV.

"Semen is supposed to be clear. Period blood is supposed to be light red. The barium is drawn to the reproductive organs, all the blood in your body ends up in your balls," he says. "Most people think it's the brain, but it's not. Your balls are the hardest-working organs. And the barium sterilizes them, and the dead tissue gets expelled. Same thing happens in women's pussies."

I am trying to avoid his eyes, because every time I meet them I hear him say, *I'm going to kill you*, without moving his mouth — the noise creaks into my head from underneath, and I know he is saying it, I know that the words are darting across his brain. He is talking and talking, but in his brain, he is strangling me, dissecting me, cutting my throat, shooting me in the head. He is telling me, so he can get me scared. He is saying, *I'm going to kill you, I'm going to inhabit you.*

He says, "You know where else it's used?"

"What?" I ask.

"Barium."

"No."

He motions over to the bottles of camper fuel sitting by the door. Dried and empty, their thick taste still lingering in my cheeks and coating my tongue.

"It's all in that shit we've been shooting all day," he says, and I can smell the sex in the trailer, the mildew on the towels in the bathroom, and I can even smell the TV, the cracked glass of the windows. I hear his under-voice in my head, *The things in this world send signals.*

I leave as fast as I can, and even with my back turned I hear it, *The deadest metals and the softest woods, they talk when you're not around.* They talk in words that correspond directly to things; words that sit as labels in the Platonic museum of meaning, that denote perfectly and connote nothing. Free from the confusion of context, they beam messages back and forth always, divine signals in a network of pure communion. As soon as I cross the threshold of the trailer, I run back down the line toward the shed, but it's dark out again, and I didn't see that coming, and as I move through the dark, I hear his voice, chthonic and murmuring, *The world is a brain. Electric and aware. Hell is real.*

I miss the last bus, so I go down to the woods by the river near his place to wait until the morning buses start running again, and I dig a hole and set one of the candles. I shoot more ice and stare at the flame, grinding my teeth, reading a paperback, slapping at the mosquitoes, jumping at every noise and movement, possum feet on the leaves and gleaming raccoon eyes in the ether as I try to jerk off to a crumpled-up *Club* magazine. I feel someone with me in the vibrating candlelight, I feel him nudge my arm to scoot me over so he can see the magazine, so its images can reveal to him what they do to me. He mirrors my movements in the shadows, and he remains as quiet as my silhouette while the dank, interstitial forest whistles in the night wind and transmits — in its direct and objective language — *the world is the world, and no one ever leaves.*

Each day is itself squared. The hallucinations and delusions multiply by themselves. 2×2, 3×3, 4×4, etc. I am moving on the bus in a Cartesian triangle. The shed about six miles west of the trailer park, the library seven miles southeast of the trailer park. The shed four miles north of the library. With Florida Ave. as the y-axis and the library as the origin $(0,0)$, the shed is $(0, 4)$ and the trailer park is $(6, 4)$. Then the slope is $6/4$, and I can find anywhere along this line, the trailer park–library line, all the way out to the east coast. All the way down through the Gulf. Everything, everything that seems like a triangle is actually just a circle, or, rather, a triangle is only a triangle in relation to a circle. Descartes knew that. Plato knew that. The wrestler knew it. Now I do, too.

At the library downtown, I get a computer facing the wall. I take another half of a Viagra and let the dark stuff outside of sight contract and make my field of vision narrow. And I watch porn for a really long time. I watch porn until everything is raw. I watch porn until people start to notice and the fear makes me soft and then the porn makes me hard and then the fear makes me soft and then a woman clears her throat in front of me and says, "What are you doing?"

And I leave the library.

I go to a 7-Eleven and get a forty to try to take the edge off, but it doesn't work. The edge stays, and the liquor just makes it sharper, washes it clean. The sun is scarring my eyes. I can feel the white parts getting burned and hard, and my toes are itching and sweating, and the athlete's foot I picked up in some institution shower is spilling out and blooming, replicating all across my right foot like ivy. I want to rip the skin off, to use my nails and just peel it all back and expose the clean meat. I go back into the gas station and I walk to the single bathrooms, and the men's room is taken, so I go into the women's. I lock the door, and I take out the bottle cap in my pocket, and I fix a shot on the foldout baby-changing table, and I shoot it into the puffy vein that lives on top of the ball of my ankle, and I deflate onto the toilet, my jeans against the plastic toilet seat, and I cough that weak little meth cough and feel all my juice rush to my head, and I open my jaw a few times and look around the tile room that just seems to get brighter, and I try to get my bearings, but by now the hallucinations have really started to set, to become a constant chatter, like turning the knob on a radio out in the country, mostly interference and then something becomes clear for a moment, and I start to think that this is just the background noise of life as I know it, that it actually isn't new, the lack of sleep is just making me forget how to tune it out, and I'm helpless against it, so I just try to listen, and my head is talking about how I need to eat, but my stomach isn't hungry, and it's saying this lack of communication is gonna kill me, it's saying, *Neuro-corporeal miscommunication, that's what the coroner's report will say, a brain that can't talk to its own stomach, speaking different languages and lost in translation is how we are gonna die, that's a medical term, neuro-corporeal miscommunication, a diagnosis in the* DSM-8, *which will come out in 2035, and the coroner who gets our body slapped down onto his table will be the first to discover it, he will study our guts and our brain and publish a 500-page paper and he will get a whole new diagnosis named after him and he's gonna change the landscape of how we perceive psychosomatic illness; we will be a famous medical oddity, students across the country will study the files for decades, but for now let's try to get hungry, let's think about the Dollar Menu: the McDouble, the McChicken, a cold Sprite, breakfast, sausage breakfast, hotcakes, biscuits and circular eggs, salty hot fries, apple pies, McNuggets dipped in honey, just go stand by the drive-thru window and time it up nice, wait for a car to be a little too far from the window, and get down in a three-point stance and Usain Bolt through the gap, grab the bag, and don't look back, just run somewhere cool and eat — eat, goddamnit — you got no blood in your body, it's all in your head,* but all this talk about food is making me nauseous and there is a knock on the bathroom door that makes me jump. I leave and stare at the ground as I shuffle past the woman who is waiting.

I go back to the library (0,0), I go back to the shed (0,4), I ride the bus, I go back and buy ice in the raised trailer (6,4) and talk about chemtrails, perfect asses, licks to hit, and what's next, I go back to the library and jerk off on the computer, watching gigabytes of porn, falling down hyperlink holes and scrabbling out and looking for another — pregnant, trans, gay, straight, old, young, amateur, professional, I steal Neosporin from the CVS and put it on my scraped dick, I bite down on my teeth so hard I think I feel the muscles under my ear explode from the pressure, I bite holes in my cheeks and on my tongue, and I don't say anything — when I talk it's quiet and strained, hoarse, I just listen, listen to the chorus in my head say, *Look at him go, look at him go, our little ricochet, our little bullet bouncing and bouncing,* only that's not what I really hear, what I really hear are voices I don't recognize say shit like, *All right, after he turns that corner I'm gonna grab him, I'll put his head against the wall and you run his pockets,* and so I turn around to see who's planning to do what to me and, of course, they're quick, quicker than me, and they hide in that millisecond that I turn 180, and so I pick up my pace, and I see McKay's car everywhere I go, that gray Impala with the lights on, dark windows, and idle. *Hell is real. The world is a brain.*

I'm in uncharted territory on the sixth day, never awake that long, and I feel like snagged fishing line, taut and still. I am seeing the continuity of days, the artificiality of night, that arbitrary black break, not a monolithic thing to sleep through but something with phases. I see the moon move like the sun, the crowds change in the night, and in that last transitory phase of dark, dark morning, the low single digits that creep higher with every passing moment, I stand in the middle of a residential street in Bruce's quiet little neighborhood.

The hours are hot and wet like breath, the fog is thick, and I am between two streetlamps whose light doesn't travel; it stays stuck around them in a ball, hemmed in by the heavy mist. The telephone wires above me are buzzing, crackling. I am acutely aware of their electricity. I stand in the middle of the road and stare at the row of cars stretching out in front of me; the fog is rolling across the street and the front yards of the old one-story bungalows, rolling up onto their porches and caressing the wood and the sideboards, the painted windowpanes and the cold dark glass. Three and a half cars are visible before my vision is eaten by the cloud, and I start trying doors.

Locked.

Locked.

Locked.

Locked.

Hands on the wet window trying to see what I can see. There is a BMW with a briefcase in the back, a gym bag, some clothes, but it's locked.

Locked.

Locked.

Open. The dome light comes on and I act quick. I let the fog in, and I steal all the quarters and shove them in my pocket, I look in the glove box and the middle console: papers and garbage and an owner's manual, I steal the dimes. There is dry cleaning hanging from a hook on the back seat, I rip the film off of it and take the suit off the wire hanger, it's too big for me, and I bundle it up and stick it under my arm. I take the hanger and I get out of the car. I close the door, my head still talking, saying, *Heavy pants, what are you gonna do with all those dimes, heavy pants.*

I go to the porta potty and put the suit down. I prop the door open and wait for the dome light in the car to go off. I wait. A van drives by throwing newspapers at stoops. I let it pass and I rip the paper off the hanger. I untwist it into a straight wire, and I go back to the BMW with the briefcase and I jiggle the lock. It takes some doing, but I do it. And as the alarm starts blaring, I move fast. I grab the briefcase and the gym bag, I look in the middle console: a watch, in the glove compartment: a gun, a 9mm Glock in a holster, and my head says quick and forceful, *Blow your brains out right here, coward,* and it's heavy in my hand and the alarm is making my heart beat irregular. *Let them find you like this, half in, half out, with your brains all over the dash, heavy pants.* I put the gun, the watch, and the suit in the gym bag, I grab the briefcase, too, and a handful of change, and I run back to Bruce's with the car alarm in my ears and my pants heavy on my hips.

As the sun rises, I examine my haul. The gun is new, a beautiful instrument in and of itself, a work of art. Economical and organized, and every time I look at it that voice in my head says, *Do it, pussy.* So I hide it, and I examine the suit. It seems normal, but maybe it's expensive. In the gym bag is another watch, I look at both of them, one gold and one silver, both heavy like the gun. Names I sort of recognize. In the briefcase, a laptop. I hope for a credit card, a company card or something, but nothing. The laptop is new and sleek and a Mac, and I open it but it's password protected, so I put it back in the briefcase.

When it seems late enough in the morning, I pack everything into the gym bag, and I go to Publix and dump the coins in the Coinstar machine and I get a ten, a five, and a one. I go to a pawn shop down Hillsborough on the (0,4) (6,4) line, and I sell the briefcase and the laptop and the watches. He inspects the watches and then me, and I say, "My father passed," in a way that sounds like a lie, and his eyebrows move a little, and he looks back at the watches. I do a little bit of haggling, trying to find my footing in the negotiation, but he bowls me over. My nerves are shot and I'm lucky to be able to make a sentence.

He says, "I can get an appraiser to give an official quote, but we will need to see some documentation." He knows that this is his angle, this appraiser. He knows I'll never let that happen. He has on a black and gold hat that says VETERAN and VIETNAM or GULF WAR or one of those above it. I walk out of the store and get scared by the bell over the door, my pants a little lighter. I traded the laptop for $300, $150 for the gold watch, $80 for the silver one, and $20 for the briefcase. I was too nervous to bring up the gun.

I get a motel room, and I use the phone to call a woman I know who sells crack, and she comes over in a wifebeater and a flat-brimmed hat, and we smoke it and touch each other and watch game shows with the curtains drawn. She tells me that I don't look so good, and she sits on my face until I can't breathe, and I come sweating into the seventh day.

I realize that I didn't go to Bruce's to see if McKay came by. I look at the clock radio and it says seven, that rare hour that looks the same both ways, morning and evening. Transitionary.

I want this run to end. As I am trying doors on the street, I am, underneath, hoping and screaming that they would all be locked. That I would come up empty-handed and be completely flat broke again. That the ground would disappear underneath me, and I would be swallowed up by the fatigue. So I could finally get some rest. I could have at least a day of resolution, of swearing that I am done for good, that I will never do it again. That this was it, the last time. But, no luck, the gun is still in the gym bag with the crumpled-up suit.

The gun is a decision. The gun could end this run once and for all, permanent and without question, or it could prolong it. It could be an endless source of revenue. Or I could sell it, could probably get close to five hundred bucks for it. And then, what? The run goes on for more days. More and more days. But it's heavy and it's beautiful, and I feel the smooth stock and the plug of the safety, the squared barrel like a long hallway.

A few years before, a guy I knew accidentally shot himself on someone else's couch. He used to sell blues, and he was fucked up. He was just sitting there handling the gun, holding it probably like I am holding the Glock, feeling it, and it went off in his hand. *Pop,* and the wet matter of his brain exploded. He wasn't alone, there were other people in the room, there was even someone sitting right next to him on the couch. To hear them describe it, it's spooky. Normal day, normal con-versation, and then — like a sudden shout — matter. That's what fucked them up: the matter, the residue, the everything all over the walls. Seeing the stuff you weren't supposed to see, the stuff that's supposed to stay upstairs, in the attic, in between the ears, his hopes and dreams and loves and hates just sprayed across the wallpaper. Everything that made him him.

How does a gun just go off? He must have pulled the trig-ger. But I have heard about this from time to time, these accidents, someone cleaning the gun, waving it around, pretending. Sitting there, holding the Glock and feeling its magnificent heaviness, I start to think that maybe it was a Freudian slip of the finger. Not that he wanted to die, but maybe that's what his hand wanted. Or that's what the gun wanted, and it convinced his hand while he was just sitting there talking to someone else, staring at the TV, distracted.

I think about all the things I can't coerce. The forces of accident and chance and predestination. The winds that blow me around. All of them talking and planning when I'm not around.

I put the gun back in the bag and recycle the day, I go back to the library (0,0), I go back to the shed (0,4), I ride the bus, I go back and buy ice in the raised trailer (6,4), and I think about pulling the gun on the cook as he rambles about chemtrails and perfect asses. I go back to the library and wake the computer from its screensaver dreams, I let the blue light mirror the blue light in my mind, let the porn reflect the porn in my head, jumping genres and traveling down the hyperlink holes of my brain — pregnant, trans, gay, straight, old, young, amateur. I go to the bathroom and smear Neosporin on my scraped dick, take off my busted shoes and smear Lotrimin on my toes, itching under a blanket of fungus. I bite down on my teeth so hard I can hear them scream, beg me to stop, and I bite holes in my cheeks and on my tongue, and feel my mouth turn sour with tiny life, and I don't say anything — when I talk it's quiet and strained, hoarse, and I steal a Gatorade and try to lubricate the dry tendons in my neck, and I feel the acid rushing up from my stomach, and I just listen, listen to the chorus in my head say, *Look at him go, look at him go, our little ricochet, our little bullet bouncing and bouncing on the walls of the skull of the world*, only that's not what I really hear, what I really hear is voices I don't recognize say shit like, *All right, after he turns that corner I'm gonna grab him, I'll put his head against the wall and you snatch the life out of his pockets, take his shoes,* and so I turn around to see who's planning to do what to me and, of course, they're quick, quicker than me and they hide in that millisecond that I turn 180, and so I pick up my pace, and I hear the gun taunting me, calling me names, and I see McKay's car everywhere I go, that gray Impala with the lights on, dark windows, and idle. *The world is real. Hell is a brain.*

By the early morning, I am back in the shed, and I still have the gun bound and gagged in the gym bag, and I am unscrewing Bruce's lawn mower, piece by piece, undoing it and passing each little part through the window, the handle broken into four parts, the plastic body I have to slide diagonally to fit, the engine, the bag folded up, the gas tank, the blade, the lever to open the bag. I break the machine into tiny digestible parts, and I put the screws and washers into my pocket and let the rest of the pieces land in the dirt of the alley with a slight bounce.

I look at the pile of dismantled pieces, and then I go through the window, and I sit in the dirt, and I put it back together, build it back from nothing. It is all so intricately complex, and I remember each component, where each part goes according to its use and its design. This takes me an hour or so, I would guess, but then I have the mower, tall and complete, as if I had just passed it through the window in its pure form, and I wheel it down the street, I cross the crowded road pushing it with one hand, in the other the toolbox and the gym bag. The traffic noise is unbearable. I push it to a different pawnshop, and I sell the mower and the toolbox, the bag and the gun sitting at my feet. I get $100 for both, which is better than I was expecting, even though the mower has never been touched.

The money is gone in a few minutes, and I am sitting there on the couch in my dealer's trailer, and I am holding the Glock, I am turning it in my hand and thinking about the Freudian slip and the everything that spills out afterward. *The brain is real. The world is a hell.* I am talking about how new it is, popping out the clip and showing the bullets, engaged in some fast, hoarse sales pitch that has been lodged in my throat for days.

I go back to the library, 7.2 miles southwest, to the corridors of dead minds frozen onto paper and stacked in neat rows. I feel them calling to me like ghosts in the night, I read their thoughts without opening their books; I just pace and sit in the rows on the second floor. I go back to the bathroom, shoot up, and brace my hands on the sides of the stall. I look for something, anything to read, and I feel my body like a bastard amalgamation, mismatched and jerky, a union of spare and random parts. I ride the bus, I go back and buy ice in the raised trailer and talk about chemtrails, perfect asses, talk to the under-voice, and come up with licks to hit and what's next, and somewhere in the jabbering I feel myself dying from starvation, on the couch and in the talking, I feel the organs inside my chest accelerate, age exponentially and wither and die, and I go back to the library and jerk off on the computer, watching as much porn as I can, until I don't know my own name, jumping genres like a frantic conversation you lost control of, falling down hyperlink holes and scrabbling out and looking for another — pregnant, trans, gay, straight, old, young, amateur — trying to get my mind to snap back into place, and I try to jerk off in my pants, but I am completely soft and completely absent. I bite down on my teeth so hard I feel every individual molecule in my gums groan and strain under the pressure. I bite holes in my cheeks and on my tongue and feel them fester and bleed and get invaded by tiny foreign squirming bacteria, kicking their million legs in circles and wagging their tails burrowing into my head, and I don't say anything, when I talk it's quiet and strained, hoarse, as if my voice is sick and dying, outlived its purpose, and I just listen, listen to the chorus of the dead in the library that follows me out into the world onto the bus and on the streets saying, *Look at him go, look at him go, our little ricochet, our little bullet bouncing and bouncing,* only that's not what I really hear, what I really hear is voices I don't recognize say shit like, *All right, after he turns that corner I'm gonna grab him, I'll put his head against the wall and you run his pockets. Run, boy, you better run. Run home and don't ever come back. You better run into the ocean and sink to the bottom, to where the sun never shines and die, die there or else,* and so I turn around to see who's planning to do what to me and they are there, the people of the world, staring at me and shooting these thoughts into my brain through their eyes, and all the shadows are taking form, too, and turning into more people and more stares, and a crowd is forming everywhere I go, running chatter, and if they talk so much, if they're so smart, why don't they just get it over with. And I pick up my pace, and I see McKay everywhere I go, I feel the dual ends of my life simultaneously, prison and death, and I feel my eyes red cracked behind the yellow scars, I feel them drying and losing their purpose, I run from the sun, singular and powerful, beating hard and discriminatory on me, *Hell is real,* and I run from the shadows, the endless and evil multiplicity of their secret forms, *The world is a brain,* diseased by repetitive thoughts.

And, on that eighth day, if I am only a thought in the mind of God, then I must be a symptom of his mental illness. The thought that blossoms into an idea that drives him mad. His true power, a consciousness that can think thoughts that have their own lives, their own unique thoughts. And so, to fall prey to madness is to drive God mad. To live as I was, vibrating in a sleepless bender, was to be a source of extreme ecstasy and debilitating pain for God. I get the sense that people are the agents through which God becomes fallible, subject, as we are, to misinformation and destruction.

In the creation of our world machine, I think, even God couldn't avoid friction, couldn't avoid erosion and the gradual breakdown and loss of energy. Each interaction between each little thing in the world, each thought and each brush, brings the wheels of the machine closer to their grinding halt. Each loses a minuscule amount of energy that over billions of years will total the sum finite energy of the whole project, and so the early world must have been close to perfect, that primitive simmer that boiled over and evaporated itself.

Or maybe it isn't that he couldn't avoid friction, but that it is there by design, the world a clever plan by which God could kill himself, an intricate suicide machine played out over eons. He baked in a self-destruct mechanism to skirt and deny his own omnipotence. Or maybe that isn't right, because if he created it, then he must be beyond his creation, so maybe the world is just God self-harming, trying to make himself feel by raking a razor across his skin.

Either way, I knew my life was the duration of a thought exhausting itself, and I could feel the thought running out of steam, trailing off like a comet through a dead-ended electric pathway.

I was the thought that never formed a connection, never linked up to new pathways, and never caused anything of consequence. I was a spasm, a brain zap, and I knew it. Pointless and fleeting, involuntary. A symptom perhaps of some kind of excess heavenly epinephrine in God's brain. I was born a loose mental flare, a stray thought that he needed to hammer down, to contextualize in a web of meaning.

And if I am a thought created in his image, then my own thoughts must be made in the image of myself, imperfect inversions of my own consciousnesses, and if I am a mortal god, a god who shits and decays and is closing in on his own death, a creator who is subject to destruction, then what type of double-mortal, double-shitting character do my thoughts have? What kind of double death will my thoughts die after their abbreviated lives, what do they leave behind in the toilet bowls of their tiny world, my tiny brain? How soon until they finally expend all of my finite energy and drop me dead in my own tiny world? The answer felt right at hand.

And somewhere on that last day, my heart begins to feel like an old door on rusted hinges getting slammed open and shut, and with each creaking slam my chest feels smaller, and I can feel my eyes start to shake, and I start to hear about things I have no business hearing about. Voices talking over one another, arguing about whether or not I am gonna die, and I am in that little tin shed by the alley that had become my home, only the sun is out and beating through the tiny window, and it is hot in there, hot like the earth, and the door in my chest keeps slamming and getting rustier and more painful, and my eyes are getting shakier, the noises in my head getting louder. I would say what my stomach is doing, but I think it is gone.

And then my vision goes slow and slow and shuts off like an old cathode-ray TV, everything starts ringing and then it shuts, just sucks into the middle, slow, fast, and white, then a blip.

My body seizes and I fall to the ground, bleeding from the head, spasming on the floor, my fingers tracing unconscious circles in the dirt, and my sneaker scraping across the ground like I am trying to push myself forward, making a sound like bushes in the wind; from my mouth, a strained clicking like a broken pilot light, a dead car battery on the ocean floor.

*   *   *

I came to on Bruce's couch.

"David," he said. His eyes were welling.

"David." His hands were cupping my jaw.

"How do you feel?" His palms were on my cheeks, his fingertips on my temple.

He gave me a few of his Klonopin and I fell into a dreamless, amniotic sleep on his couch.

12

I DON'T KNOW HOW LONG I SLEPT, but I woke up
feeling taller. All the faraway voices and shadows were gone,
and I walked to the kitchen and drank water from the faucet. Bruce came in and asked me again how I felt. He wasn't
wearing his work clothes, and I wondered if it was the weekend or if he just called in sick. I noticed that he seemed different since he had moved. More nervous, less extravagant, less
of that high drama that I always got a kick out of. He was just
regular, concerned.

We went to an ice cream parlor, a walk-up window with a
soft-serve machine and a few picnic tables out front. I got a
vanilla cone dipped in chocolate, and I scarfed it down, and
Bruce bought me another. We sat at the picnic tables in the
sun and the breeze and, as I bit pieces off the chocolate shell,

I listened to Bruce talk, him on the bench and me sitting on the table with my feet on the bench.

"I was checking on you every night before I went to sleep," he said. "I heard you clamoring around back there one night. I thought you were a raccoon."

I tried to place everything chronologically, so I could figure out how long I was out on the ground and how long I slept on the couch. But I gave up and just took the ice cream cone slow.

"I knew something like this was gonna happen. I had a premonition," he said. All of the chocolate was gone now, and I was working on the smooth, cold dairy. I could feel the calcium and the sugar hitting my bloodstream. My body was so grateful it was practically crying.

Bruce was sipping on a strawberry milkshake, and the sun was beginning to set; it was pink and gold out, both the sun and the moon visible in the pale blue sky. There was a flock of short green parrots on the telephone wires trilling and flapping over the traffic on the street.

He said, "I've been reading again."

I nodded.

"Not just the AA book, either. Everything. Sobriety isn't so bad. It's actually pretty nice. I feel like I am finally getting to know myself."

There was an owl in a tree somewhere nearby. I could hear it waking up, getting ready for night. I wondered what Bruce and I looked like. Father and son? Maybe stepfather — him, tall and dusty blond, and me, me.

"I need a shower," I said. I was on the cone now, my favorite part.

"There are girls," he said. "You know, at the meetings."

"Yeah, I've been before. I know there's girls."

"I could get you into a treatment center, at least a halfway house. The Salvation Army," he said.

I finished the bottommost part of the cone and lay down across the top of the table. I stretched my whole body out and yawned.

"You know I won't last," I said.

"You could try."

"Bruce, I can't think about this right now. I need a shower. And some real food." I hung my head upside down off the back of the table and felt the blood rush to it.

"There are other people in the world, David. You pretend there aren't, but there are. When's the last time you talked to your family?"

"I don't know. Do you still smoke?"

"I'm trying to quit," he said, as he took out a pack of Marlboro Menthols. They were long and light, and he put one in my hand, and I lit it upside down, the mint mixing with the thick taste of ice cream and chocolate still on the back of my tongue.

"OK. So say I go to treatment," I said. "What do I tell my PO?"

"I'm sure he would understand. It's better than the alternative."

"I've done it before. I've done this all before. Seized and

come back. Tried to stop and failed. Gone to meetings. It's just noise." Upside down, I looked at the blue and pink sky on the ground and the street on the ceiling, up past my eyeline.

"You've never really tried," he said.

"How long has it been for you? Since you've been clean?"

"Seven months," he said. "Don't change the subject."

"This is the subject," I said. "You really think you're done? Like done done? Come on."

He looked at his milkshake.

"You're fucked just like me, Bruce. We both know it. It's me, not your sponsor. You'll be buying my piss in three months."

"I'm sorry," he said under his breath.

"You'll be paying me to let you blow me. To get me to jerk you off. Ninety days, mark it."

"I'm sorry," he said, louder this time.

"You don't have to apologize to me. I get it. Believe me. If anyone gets it, I get it. We're brothers of the same long night."

I shifted my head onto the picnic table and bent my elbow and rested my head in between my right wrist and my bicep. I smoked with my left hand. Bruce, on the bench, couldn't sit still. He was fidgeting with his straw and his spoon and the remnants of his strawberry milkshake. We sat there in silence for a little, listening to the dull idling of engines on the street, the early calls of the owl, the parrots swarming together with their long and sharp tails, flapping in short, sporadic bursts from palm tree to telephone wire. There were bats now, too, flying and hunting in their erratic way, tracking bugs with radar in the pale dusk.

"You've gotta come out of that shed eventually, David.

You've gotta interact. You can't spend your whole life locked in that little dark room, in your little dark head."

"I want a lobotomy. Do they still do lobotomies?" I asked.

"No."

"Well, they should. I want one."

Bruce put his hand on my shoulder. I realized that I didn't remember going from the shed to the couch, that I probably couldn't walk, and he must have carried me.

"What about shock treatment?" I asked.

"Yeah, I think they still do that," he said. "But not at the Salvation Army."

"Well, then I'm fucked," I said.

We sat like that for a while, Bruce with his hand on my shoulder, me finishing the ends of the long cigarette, staring at the moon getting subtly brighter in the darkening blue sky, watching leaves fall out of trees. His hand was warm and heavy, like an anchor in the summer sea.

"I want a Big Mac," I said. "Get me a Big Mac, and I'll let you lecture me for as long as you want."

Bruce set me up in his guest room. I was tired but thirsty, and I went to drink more from the kitchen sink, the old floors creaking under my feet. There were still a few lights on, but I didn't want to knock anything over or wake up Bruce. As I walked past his bedroom, through his cracked door, I saw him kneeling at the foot of his bed. I could hear him speaking, quiet and under his breath, holding a book in front of his face. I only heard the end of what he was reading, but I really couldn't believe what he was doing: Bruce, the intellectual, Bruce, the rich, disdainful meth-crazed, middle-aged ghoul, on his knees at the foot of his bed like a schoolboy saying prayers before bed: "Lord, grant that I may seek rather to comfort than to be comforted, to understand, than to be understood, to love, than to be loved. For it is by self-forgetting that one finds. It is by forgiving that one is forgiven. It is by dying that one awakens to Eternal Life. Amen."

He sat in silence for a moment, and then he continued, "And please, if it's your will, help David. Help me to help him. Help him to heal. Grant him . . ." He paused. "Help him accept help."

There, with my bare feet on the cool hardwood, I thought about my brother and me in our room, our dad standing in the doorway watching us as we said our prayers, as we said thank you for the day, as we prayed like he taught us, prayed for our grandparents and our uncle, for anyone we knew who was sick, for the dead, for them to be happy and together in heaven. For the old man we drove to church some Sundays, who was too old and too short to drive and so would walk for miles in the heat in a suit and hat to the church downtown, who was sick and alone; for the homeless men that my brother and I would see by the Little League field or by the bay, and who we had just recently started to notice, who would scare us and make us sad, who I would sometimes have nightmares about — we would pray for all these people, and there, on the hardwood, it occurred to me that we never prayed for ourselves, that I didn't ask for toys or for something good to happen to me, we just expressed our love to the dark, we threw it out into the night and the world and hoped that it would land where it was supposed to go.

But sometimes I would keep the prayer going for a few seconds longer, and I would ask for something for myself, I would ask for God to please let me into heaven when I died, to let me be with my family there and not alone somewhere else. And I would think, but never ask, why, why did he choose me to be a part of this world, to be thrust out here, a part of humanity, a limb on this deranged tree, one of the elected souls. And then my dad would walk over to our beds, one by one, our twin beds touching opposite walls and say, "Te quiero mucho," and kiss us on the cheek.

And I felt again that God, if there was one, would have to have a little bit of me within him. No, not a little bit, all of me. All of my tics and neuroses. My love of the floor, of the quietness of parts of the world, my relentlessly circular brain, he would have to have that within himself, be confused and circular and full of preferences, too, in order to create it. And even if it wasn't God, the fact that I am here, in Bruce's house and in time, makes these things real, somehow connected, somehow begat. And if my life is full of days, then what are my days full of if not life?

Bruce let me stay at his place until I could piss clean, then he called and got me a bed in the same halfway house I had just left but in a different room. Somewhere along the way, a few months in, my sponsor convinced me to get a cell phone. I felt primitive holding it in my hand, a little flip phone like I had when I was younger, poking the keys like a monkey, wide-eyed as I shuffled through the letters spelling them out one by one. I got scared of it, scared of its silent signals and everything it represented, the new normal. The life of a citizen, gadgeted and content, a deep, measurable connection with the vast networks of the world that pulsed over my head. And even though I trusted my sponsor, I kept the phone in the bedside drawer most of the time, locked in the bureau so it couldn't hurt me.

Early on, deep into those nights where I was tormented by waking cocaine dreams, twitching in my bed in the halfway house, I would open the blinds and let the moonlight onto my skin, that other sun that rose in defiance of the first, that snuck out behind his back, I would let its light touch my bed and my eyes, and I would think of the life ahead of me. I would think that I had never done anything worth doing, and I couldn't conceive of a situation where I ever would. From that post of immense self-pitying, the enveloping subjectivity of the mind of an abstinent addict, I observed the cycles that dictated my life, the binges and the crashes and the middle times, Dr. Greg's charts made tangible, but I observed them from the bed, from inaction. I felt the feelings that stirred me into the night, but I didn't go. I was paralyzed in the bed, and my roommate had just relapsed and been kicked out, so I had the room to myself. The twin bed sitting under the window across from me, the mattress bare and empty, stained from the sweat of the post-acute withdrawals of a hundred lost bodies, disharmonious and bubbling over like bad chemistry experiments. By 2 a.m. the desire for drugs morphs into the other familiar desire, for silence and senselessness, the desire to be eaten by the swamp of nothingness, and again I couldn't recall ever doing anything worth doing.

I could see the night unfolding in that familiar pattern, hours of simple, charged thoughts — the image of needle and plunge over and over — morphing into terrible abstraction. But it was just beginning, so I tried to head it off, to reach back into something from before. I reached for my phone in the drawer and called my ex-girlfriend, the ten digits made permanent in my brain a long time ago. She answered. My number was new, but she recognized me as soon as she heard me.

"Nicole" — my voice, familiar, slow, and creaky whenever I first coaxed it out of its hiding place.

"Where are you?"

I told her. I told her specifically where I was, where my thoughts were, and where the moon was. I told her about the nights, the long torturous nights of these early days and the thoughts and images I couldn't get out of my head. How I couldn't decide what was what, how I had no footing in this world, and how I just wanted to push the reset button on my life. I wanted to ask her to put her phone in her closet, to let me hear her quiet, pretty garden, but I knew she wasn't home. She had moved to college, to a dorm room somewhere, and I could hear voices in the background, and I could hear distraction in her voice as she half listened to my frazzled pleas. I heard her put her hand over the phone and say something to the people she was with.

"Now really isn't a good time," she said back into the phone, "but I'm glad you're getting help"—these words thick with disillusionment, laden with the memories of all the previous "help" that clattered around in my head without ever falling into place. Tears started ripping down my cheeks, fast, faster than the sunset evenings. Tears not of anxiety or fear of some looming horror, but tears of understanding that the horror was already here, tears of guilt and shame, of finality and con-nection, as if two wires were brought together to start some previously unknown engine in my face, that kick-started my eyes and my sinuses, and I moved to the empty bed, to crack open the window and light a cigarette, and the angle from which I smoked sent tears down the side of my head and into my ears, filling them and dripping down onto the mattress; tears filling my mouth and my nose and making it hard to breathe and wetting the filter of my cigarette, stopping the smoke from pulling, and I thought of her, wherever she was, probably holding the phone a safe distance away from her ear to stop my tears from filling it, too.

She said, "Have you talked to your family? Maybe you should call your brother."

And my sobs kept running over the dead energy of the phones, silence on both ends except for my struggled breath-ing, as the minutes stretched on until she finally said, "I have to go. Call your brother."

And she hung up, but the phone stayed flipped open while the engine idled all night long, and I fell asleep on the empty, itchy mattress, soaked it through like so many other people had done. The sleep was like the one at Bruce's, and when I woke up, I started carrying my phone with me hoping she would text me or call me back. It was heavy and uncomfortable in my pocket, emitting its silent signals. Guys started to come up to me after meetings and type their numbers into it. They'd call themselves, so they had my number, and then they used it. Called me up at all hours and just asked about my day, what was going on. So, I unwittingly started to populate the device with friends and acquaintances; I started to see the circle radiate out from me, a network of lives and basic, uncomplicated relationships. The one hundred fifty. Everyone's names in the address book followed by the same designation, "AA," as if there was anyone else, any other group to designate. I did call my brother, eventually, and further on my sister, my other brother, the nieces and nephews — I went to their school plays and their T-ball games; I went to their elementary school graduations. They understood me immediately, my siblings, they didn't require anything of me, their kids were the same way. Everyone was just happy to hear from me. Finding my footing back in the family, my place as the little brother, the young uncle, was easy, fun to cheer at the baseball games and open presents on Christmas.

And when the time came, I would make the harder calls, to my mom, my dad. Over time, I started putting my number into other people's phones, looking into the bewildered eyes of some young kid just showing up at a meeting for the first time, telling him to call me whenever, telling him I'm up all night, and then calling him and asking about his day.

My GED comes in the mail. I clean up like a fish gets hooked, just going about my life and then dragged somewhere else. I pass days in monotony and normalness. Those few months of sobriety stretching into the teens, and I start to go to school, community college, then transfer to a university, and I start telling myself that I want to be a doctor, but if the legal shit gets in the way, I will try to become a marine biologist, which I figure is less strict. I am a healthy weight. I am well-rested, but still nervous and jumpy for a year, scared of the classes and the foreign, sudden noises, moving like a prey animal, staying close to walls and passing my eyes across everything, waiting for something to come and get me.

I test out of the freshman English and math classes, but I still feel older than my peers, much older despite it really being only two or three years. It feels like decades, like I went to space, to some distant planet where time galloped at ten times its normal speed, and then I came back to Earth, where the sun rises and sets slowly, where the days and lives drag on and ooze across your mind. I show back up, creases in my face, deep-set wrinkles, and skin spotted with age, with the mental lapses of a grandparent, hair falling out, and I take my place back in line, slip into the classroom of life after a brief absence. And yet, in the classroom there are other students with other lives, and maybe some of them have been to other planets, too, maybe some even more distant, where time moved even faster.

I was taking a Faulkner seminar, a Kant seminar, biology, lab, and a weird small class called "Religion and Ecology." My professor would talk about global destruction, apocalypse brought on by the blind, nebulous craving in our hearts, the "climate crisis," as he called it. He blamed it initially on the

First Agricultural Revolution, where we began to develop tricks to exploit the world rather than depend on it like the hunter-gatherers, selective measures that eased the struggle of life, that led to civilizations and the gradual figuring out of the practical problems arising from them. Then he talked about the "Axial Age thinkers," a group of people who, ignorant and geographically independent of one another in China, Greece, India, North Africa, and the Middle East, over the course of a few hundred years in the late BCEs, altered the collective consciousness of the world — some Hebrew prophets and Buddha and Confucius and Plato, Zarathustra, Homer, and the anonymous authors of the Upanishads. All of these people responsible for emphasizing the primacy of man's place in the world, the transcendent glory of God or Reason or Good or Order or Forms bestowed onto us. These thinkers sought answers from the world; they wanted nature to account for itself, rather than to worship it in its divine wonder. Any veneration or respect of the world came always after respect for the Higher Order — the material world was an effect; the cause was transcendental. "Axial" meaning a turn, a shift from the primal, cosmological philosophies of old, where the natural world loomed large over our puny heads, where we prostrated ourselves before the trees and the mountains and the vast oceans and did not ask questions of them, did not seek to understand them, worshipped them solemnly and full of fright. These Axial thinkers thought with arrogance; they opened the ontological gulf between us and the world; they rended humans from nature, used our seemingly unique capacities to direct our energy to a transcendent realm. We are fundamentally different from everything else on Earth, they said, we are of different material, immaterial material, everlasting souls animating the decaying matter of our bodies. Our thinking, our language, our reason, all proof of our unique substance. Within two millennia, all of this comes to a horrifying, violent head in the marriage of the Industrial Revolution and the Protestant Reformation, the rise of ownership, of capital, divinely bequeathed unto man, the righteous suzerain of all the natural world — our ownership itself proof of our supremacy. Our taking it proof that we deserved it all along, true for the individual and for society both. Here, the Frankenstein of all human arrogance — religion, metaphysics, physical science, economics, and mechanics smelted into one destructive omni-philosophy that finally beat the planet into submission and productivity, ignorant or uncaring about the devastation of the world, which, of course, in our infinite capacity for transcendence, we forgot we were a part of. Man, the perpetual corner-cutter, the cheater who, armed with the charisma of language, is so smart that he can convince himself not to believe in the consequences of his actions.

Or, at least, that's what I got from the class. I never took notes, but I listened pretty intently.

Obviously, I thought, I couldn't judge someone who takes things without right. Obviously, I am guiltier than most, my respect for the rights of others surely less than average — for that woman on Atlantic and countless others just like her, for the owner of the Beamer, for Bruce and every drug dealer or pedestrian I ever waved a gun or a knife or a needle at, who ever had the misfortune of being near me when I needed cash, for every girl I ever lied to or led on, for every fight I ever jumped into without thought, every face I put my knuckles on, every neck I grabbed or wrapped my bony arm around, and, on a lesser note, for all the PlayStations and Xboxes and jewelry and cash stolen over the years, for my shoes, all the shoplifted candy bars and sunglasses, clothes, pills stolen out of medicine cabinets and the people left stuck with their chronic pain or anxiety, for all the Little League fields whose lights can't turn on, all the unoccupied homes that need new air conditioners. And then, most of all, my parents, my family. The abstract harms. I pushed them apart from each other. I sowed the house with blame. I razed their emotions like a bulldozer through the Amazon. Gave them hope over some communal phone in a treatment center, only to pull it away. All the stolen money paling in comparison to the hours, days, months, years of time I stole. Stretches of worry, fear, anger, confusion, and sorrow — all these negative emotions fertilized and cultivated into the bulldozed fields of their brains, those familiar emotions to anyone who has ever loved a drug addict, and the most familiar and damning of them all: self-doubt. My mom blaming my dad for being too tough with me, my dad blaming her for being too soft. But in all those worrisome hours of the night, both of them asking themselves, *Is this my fault? Did I do something wrong?* Frantically sifting through their memories, searching for a key, a moment that could unlock some insight into what happened. Of all my harms, this tops the list, and I, in true human fashion, embodied that horrible mixture of ignorance and indifference. Self-centeredness appropriately at the center of the constellation of my harms.

Step Four revealed this to me in black-and-white, and while the ninth step gets a lot of attention in popular culture — the amends process being ripe for conflict and drama — Four was the one that held my obsession: *made a searching and fearless moral inventory of ourselves.* It sent me down holes as I sat at the kitchen counter in the halfway house, using a ruler to draw columns down the pages of a spiral notebook, hunched over with the pen drying up in my aching hand, trying to list everything that was, putting the pen down and pacing around the room for a few minutes, tossing a tennis ball from hand to hand, trying to quiet everything down so I could access that understory that plays in the faraway lobes of my brain, hearing a bit and then jumping back to the notebook to transcribe it. What I couldn't figure out was, should I blame myself fully? In AA they spoke of character defects as instincts run amok, excessive but natural, immutable desires for security and nourishment. And just like it's unfair to judge the people who discovered farming, to credit them with the knowing destruction of the world when they were only trying to satisfy their own hunger, is it unfair to judge me for my own all-consuming seeking that led to the harm of everyone I cared about? Was it simply the manifestation of biological properties encoded into my body? My sponsor, that faceless acolyte of this new, old philosophy, told me, in his infinite wisdom, not to think about it. AA preached anonymity as their spiritual foundation. He told me to leave the philosophizing to the philosophers and the biology to the biologists, and to allow myself to be "a garden-variety alcoholic." No different, no more uniquely afflicted than anyone else, to instead focus on right action, to be, like Dr. Greg told me years before, "a worker among workers." He said that only through right action would I be able to gain any clarity. And by right action he usually meant service — AA service, answering the phone, giving rides to new guys, buying them food, making coffee at the meetings, setting up chairs. With prayer and meditation in between. The prescription for me, no different than for anyone else.

He told me to pray to God to remove my shortcomings without question, and then to jump back into action, to leave my questions in class.

After I wrote my inventory and went over it with him, he told me to meditate for an hour. I lay on the narrow halfway house bed and my mind ran in its typical way — jumbled and convoluted, it started to confuse me again.

An inventory is like the library, I thought. Each item meticulously recorded and ordered. The spaceless void of the mind given geography. Like the library, which sits with human thoughts made material, given height, weight, and depth. The words taking up an entire room, an entire building, massive walls of thought and feeling cascading across floors, stacked on top of one another, erected throughout every city and town. By giving it space, you can move through it according to cardinal directions, you can observe it. Like how if you unspooled the tangle of DNA in a cell it would extend for meters, or how twenty feet of intestines could be snarled into the small pit of your stomach, untangling the chaos of a single emotion can yield pages, meters of pages sometimes. A thought can extend the length of a book, more. Can extend many books, written by many authors sharing the same thought, over centuries, over countries.

I squirmed on the twin bed, looking at the clock to see if it had been an hour. It hadn't. My mind went back to its muddle.

When I look at the ocean, at the night sky, at a forest of trees, the logic is so arcane, so complex, and so simple that it is indecipherable. But I can look at a car, a chair, a house, and I can intuit certain things about it, about how it works and how it's made, because it was made from someone's mind. I can make note of the component parts and their uses and draw conclusions about them. I can establish certain principles and systems for understanding them, because they were created with the certain limited faculties of the human mind. That's how it was with the inventory. Once it's down, it can be read, it can be seen and understood, but when it is still inside your head, there is something divine about it, indecipherable and powerful. It is pre-mental. It moves you, but you don't know why.

And so, I thought, my inventory was the residue of the past. It let me know that the past is alive and well, and everything has a history, a context, and it's all part of the same thing. The library is a monument to this fact, too, that things have happened before, that the present isn't the only thing. That ghosts are real, and they move in this world, that the basic fabric of my life was just like any other, nothing special or unique about it. But history, in all of its insecurity and self-consciousness, presented itself in snapshots, distinct moments, lives, and the only problem with books is that they have covers, that they have little titles. They pronounce their assumed specificity to the world, they lie, they false advertise. And I think about the Bible, true, in some strange way, because it contradicts itself — a bunch of patched-up, contradictory manuscripts from different times and places, truths and lies and stories all mixed together, and I think the problem with the Bible is that it's too small. They never should have stopped writing it, stopped compiling it. Someone should be working right now, stripping the covers off of every book that was ever written in every part of the world, sewing all the pages together, until you have one giant thing, miles long, and that should be the real Bible. And this book would be a record and a map, a shallow signifier and a deep repository, all in one. It would assert nothing and everything. It would eliminate the violence of the "or," that butcher's cleaver, separating the loins from the ribs from the flanks from the breasts, cutting life into digestibility. This book would digest the reader. And in this horizontal library, spread out across the world times over, you would approach the text like a trough and read what is in front of you. Just what is there. No logic with which to search out an author or a title, you just walk up and look down. This inventory, I thought, was the key to me understanding myself.

The hour ran out. I said the prayer and called my sponsor like I was supposed to.

He said, "Burn it."

"What?" I said.

"The inventory. Go outside and burn it."

I couldn't believe what I heard. "I spent like three months writing that shit. We just went over it for hours."

"Yeah, I know," he said. "And now we're done with it."

"I thought it was important."

"It is important," he said, "and now go light it on fire, that's important too."

"That's not in the Book," I said.

"So what, David? Go burn it. Give it to God."

He said, "It's just words on paper."

So I went outside, and I dropped the pages on the sidewalk in shock, and I bent down, and put my lighter on them. This moral compass that I thought would guide me through the rest of my life, all of the ordered phenomena, everything that felt so important, specific to me, my horizontal Bible, my tangled-up DNA, the pages that I felt contained all the answers to all the questions about why I did what I did. On the top page, the resentment inventory, I saw my parents, my family, Bruce, Walter, Nicole and Mister, Dr. Greg and the mesmerist, my life as it was given to me. I saw that I wasn't burning my life; I was just burning paper. Something had happened in the process of writing it down and getting rid of it — internal made external made internal again — in this alchemy, internal resentment got transformed to external love, and I loved everything and everyone in those pages simply because they were there, and, as the inventory disappeared, I loved it still because I had love within me. And once it was within, it could only move out, forward, up, externally toward what I see and feel.

My old roommate came out of the house and stood next to me, looking at the pages curling and ashing, sending black smoke into the afternoon. The flames were transparent in the sunlight. And the way smoke moves through daylight, it looks like it should make a sound, so strange and new. Strange sudden things are supposed to be accompanied by a noise, but smoke just glides noiselessly across the backdrop. There's no friction there in the world of smoke, just image and afterness. He handed me a cigarette.

"You burning your fourth step?" he asked.

"Yeah."

"That shit doesn't own you anymore," he said. "How's it feel?"

"It feels good," I said.

"You gonna quit stealing my Cap'n Crunch now or what?" he asked.

13

WHEN WE GOT TO THE AMENDS, I asked my sponsor what to do with my parents. We hadn't spoken in over a year, maybe two. He told me about "living amends." How some things would take longer than others, much longer. How they couldn't be fixed with an envelope of money or a frank discussion of my wrongdoings. How these things were necessary, too, but it would take years of simply being there to repair some damage.

At first, my mom wouldn't let me in the house. She had been going to meetings, too, ones for parents of addicts, for her own sanity. She agreed to see me at a diner and, over time, even as a relationship built, we still met there a couple times a month. The first few times, it was awkward. She eyed me with reticence; if I went to the bathroom, she looked at me skeptically when I came out. But over time, to my surprise, she loosened up. And I wouldn't say things went back to the way they were, because they were never quite like this, but the dynamic switched somewhere along the way. Sitting at the table, I could see in her eyes that her dependence, the thing she was powerless over, the love for her son, it had no highs, no euphoria like mine. Her albatross of love for me was only a series of bottoms.

It was a loud, small diner, and we would talk over the banging of dishes and the other conversations. It was the kind of place where the plates were made for pictures. Everything on the menu had five ingredients and each ingredient had multiple adjectives. There was no bacon, it was applewood smoked bacon. Whole wheat pancakes with caramelized bananas and topped with Such and Such Farm blueberries and homemade whipped cream served with a side of rosemary potato hash. I felt uncomfortable in places like this, the workout moms with their yoga mats rolled up under the table, the hungover college kids in sunglasses and bright shirts, the business casual guys with Bluetooths and loafers. The loudness of it made me sweat, made me feel like someone was standing behind me, like things were bearing down on me. The diner I liked was greasier. The food looked like shit and tasted like shit, too. The pancakes and the hash browns were the same bland color, the same mushy consistency. The waitresses were old and overweight and nice, and the coffee was anonymous, weak, and watery. It was open 24/7, and it was quiet all the time, unless an NA meeting just got out or someone was in there begging for change. But I knew my mom liked this place. It occurred to me that day that she was always, in a funny way, current with the trends. She read new books and ate the right foods. She watched the right reality TV shows and called them trashy in the right way. I wondered how she kept up with all of this while she was working sixty hours a week, while she was tucked away in our little corner in Tampa. It felt like an oddity in our house, especially after my brother left, and she was stuck with me and my dad, cavemen who grunted at each other at the dinner table and spoke with hand signs; we would sit outside in the dark and smoke in silence. For the first time, I wondered what she might have been like before. Before me and before my dad. I felt like I understood something about her, something independent from me. I wished, for a second, that I could go back in time and notice this.

One day, as we sat and ate and talked for a while, it dawned on me that we didn't say anything about probation, or relapse, or my medication. We just had a normal conversation like the rest of the people in the restaurant. I told her about my classes, and she listened while I talked about all of it.

She told me, "You know, when you were a kid, I always wanted you to take more art classes."

I winced.

"No, really. You were so good."

I said, "Everyone's mom thinks that."

"That's not true," she said. "Mothers can be honest, too. We aren't oblivious all the time."

I had forgotten about the noise of the restaurant. It was where it was for everyone else, in the background.

"Your brother's drawings were not good," she said, "just

scribbles everywhere. How's that for honest? You understood space. You get that from your dad."

That was the first time in a long time I had heard her say anything positive about him, but then she broke the spell and said, "He is trying to stop drinking, you know."

"How's that going?"

"Y'know, I don't know, we'll see," she said, and she looked down at her phone. "Anyways, you had such good detail, and you knew exactly where everything needed to be. But every time I encouraged you to draw or paint more, you just said it was 'gay.'"

"I don't remember that," I said.

"It's true, you said it with such hate. You never wanted to do art because you thought it was gay."

She was laughing, a little, and she shook her head and said, "You can be so stupid."

I nodded, and we continued eating. She looked up at me and she had the beginnings of tears building at the corners of her eyes, which are, like mine, brown and green, the color and density of trees growing over one another.

"You were so peaceful," she said, "when you were a little boy. Whenever I was with you, I could feel it. Your peaceful heart."

And for my whole life, I had attributed my unbending nature to my father, and my tumultuous sensitivity to my mother — he was stone and she was water, but looking at her, I could see that I might have had it backwards. She was the Stoic who gave me the power to understand the turning of the world, to contextualize it, and, from him, I got my sentimentality, my untamable feelings, and what were his push-ups if not hysterical cries for love, and what were the tears in her eyes if not evidence of the stable, infinite ground that my entire life was built upon?

In my Faulkner seminar, Tuesdays and Thursdays, 3–4:30 p.m., the classroom was cramped; it was loud with the background noise of zippers and canvas and typing. They kept those rooms at school so cold, like jail, freezing, I guess, to kill the germs of the thousands of people who walk around touching things, breathing and sneezing. A girl in the corner typed in bursts, a frenetic five-second spree then a break, she put her hand to her mouth and studied what she wrote. A guy in the front row squirmed in his seat, clearly wanting to interject on the lecture, to bring up something he just googled. The guy next to me bounced his leg; the girl on my other side wiggled her pen up and down with her thumb and her forefinger. In the hallways, people rush, people loiter, talk, and laugh. Outside, ducks waddle across the grass, squirrels and crows dig through the garbage cans, and Evangelicals stand with signs, or yell and argue with passersby, couples hold hands, cars knock into each other in the parking lot. There is a bake sale, brownies for a dollar, there is a band practicing on a field, there are smokers and people who hold their noses when they pass them. Past campus, there is traffic and more noise, more people in more rooms; I can't see them, but I believe they are there. Down the road is county jail, Bruce's house, my parents' house, the Salvation Army, the bay, the river, my halfway house. North is subdivisions and suburbs and, past that, quiet trees.

The professor was a middle-aged woman who wore loose, patterned clothes. Every day she had a different configuration of long earrings and necklaces and layers of bracelets up and down her arm; she jangled like a skeleton while she taught, moving her arms around, pacing. She seemed to know everything about Faulkner and his words; she loved this class, and she didn't try to hide it. Unlike a lot of professors, she didn't try to analyze or teach or extract sociohistorical lessons from the books. She just seemed to bask in the problems of the story, the ugliness and the beauty, the humor and the tragedy. It really just seemed like we were in a mutual appreciation club. Sometimes, she would, in the middle of a lecture, ask someone to read a passage aloud from the night's reading and when they were done, she would just sit there, flabbergasted, and say, "Wow. Can you imagine?"

We were reading *The Sound and the Fury*, which I had read once in the library, which I had cut through on a breeze of cocaine. The rhythm of the words solved something in my brain, as if they were a sort of combination on a padlock, an incantation, a spell, that changed me for a moment, for an afternoon, and then wore off. When I stepped out of the library that day and waited for the bus, the sun was pleasant, the street noise nothing but a fact of the world, and I thought about Quentin, whom I felt a sort of kinship with. A boy swallowed by his own head, like me, lost in the forest of timeless self, solipsistic and obsessive, drawn to the past and sleepwalking into the future. He was, as I was, self-pitying and confused. And on the bus, I was struck with a consuming thought, that I wanted to talk to someone about all of this, about what I had read, about Quentin, about broken watches and water flowing under bridges like hours under years. About the way he did it, Faulkner, how he could accomplish that chain of linguistic beauty, the extended release of information and images unfolding over each other and leading to somewhere. I wanted to talk about fate and curses, and I wanted to just say, "Wow, what a strange book," to someone, and have them say something back, anything. But there was no one. There was no one in the world for me to say that to. There was no one for me to say anything to. I hadn't talked to anyone in days, I hadn't heard any voice but the distorted version of my own that lives in the folds of my brain. In this realization, there was deep sadness and a realization of how pitiful my life actually was, and out of that came terror, because I felt like if I just read it alone and never talked about it again, then it would be like I just thought it. Like the words of the book occupied the spot in my mind where thoughts usually are, and my thoughts pop and disappear like firecrackers, and I never understand them in any real way. They are just little things that come and go. And I knew that this book would disappear, too. That I would lose it forever.

The teacher called on me, she asked me to read, and she said, "David, you have such a nice reading voice."

"When the shadow of the sash appeared on the curtains it was between seven and eight o'clock and then I was in time again, hearing the watch. It was Grandfather's and when Fa-

ther gave it to me he said I give you the mausoleum of all hope and desire . . ."

My voice sounded clear and calm, grave and forceful. On the journey from my brain to my mouth, the words took a new shape, the shape of reality, of objective fact. As the air hit them, they became beautiful, the way that blood turns red the moment it touches the oxygenated air, but before, before it is blue and nebulous and creeping.

My teacher smiled at me; the rest of the class, they felt something, too. It was like a color in the air, like for a moment the lights in the room showed green, a permeating fact in time and space. This triple life of the words—the words Faulkner gave, the words I spoke, and the words they heard. The life I was given, the life I thought, and the life I lived, three dimensions—height, length, and width. All tangled up with the tripled facts of the other people in the room, tripled lives penetrating deep into nowhere and extending out into the world, bumping into one another and embracing. I rarely participated in the class discussions, but I had a part to play, I could bring the material out into the air, where we could share it together.

It was September and the afternoon storms had been coming in like clockwork for months—you could set your life to them. Clouds growing at three, that thick smell of precipitation intensifying in the air. By the time I would leave class, it was always just about to rain. It was more than the way the clouds looked—it was a feeling. And I could usually make it to my truck without getting rained on if I hurried, but I took my time leaving class that day. I packed my bag slow, and I kinda half talked to some of the other students; I was starting to feel like maybe I was a part of the group, and by the time we got to the door of the building, it was pouring outside, and I could smell the dirt, the fresh clean dirt getting churned up by the rain, and all the people from my class were milling around under the awning, waiting for the rain to let up, and we were all together in the humid air.

Someone, a guy I didn't particularly like, who was a little too excited about the whole class and the sound of his own voice, a little too excited about his leather satchel with band buttons on it, his glasses, his rarer editions of the books we were assigned, asked me if I would mind reading some stuff from the novel he was working on. He said he appreciates my comments in class; we had talked a few times on our way out of the building, and, I guess, we had developed a sort of relationship.

He said, "It's hard to explain. But if I send you the first chapter, you will get it — would you mind?"

I wanted, for a second, to look him in the eyes and say, *Fuck no.* I thought of excuses, about how busy I am with work, or how I don't have a computer, but I remembered the bus. I remembered myself and the world, and I saw in his eyes that pale blue excitement he brought into class every day, that little tic of his brain that caused him to take up half the class talking to himself, putting on a show, and where it usually annoyed me, I saw something endearing in it, something just careless and human, just, perhaps, like me.

"Yeah, sure," I said. I told him to send it over to me, and I noticed that he was actually kind of nervous before that, that his whole demeanor changed when I said okay. He seemed to relax, and I wondered, maybe he had wanted to do this earlier, had envisioned asking me for this small favor before but lost his nerve. And I was touched by the courage that took. That never, in a million years, could I summon the courage to do what he did. And I thought of what a small thing it is to ask, how ridiculous it was for me to make him feel nervous about something so small. I saw myself from the outside. Jaw clenched, eyebrows narrowed, sitting in the back of the classroom, giving him short, gruff answers every time he talked to me. For what? I didn't know. But I was happy to have this realization, and I was happy to give him the answer he wanted. And I wouldn't say that I liked him all of a sudden or looked forward to him taking up half of next class, but I wasn't bothered. In fact, my thoughts and preferences seemed to take a back seat for a second, and what was important to me was that he feel relieved in whatever way I could help him with.

"I look forward to it," I said.

He smiled and clapped me on the shoulder, and I smiled back. He walked out into the rain toward the parking lot, and I waited a few minutes for it to lighten up, and then I followed. I felt good, not in a self-satisfied way, but more like everything was just fine. That, maybe, in some small way, I was beginning to line up what I wanted to do and what I was supposed to do.

My mom saying that thing about space gave me the courage to call my old man. When I finally got through to him, I got him to meet me at an old theater downtown. It had balco-

nies and an organ and little fake gold statues by the stone pillars. It had old-school water fountains, basins with spouts,
and the seats were small and steep. The place had died and
been reborn a hundred times with the temperamental fluc-
tuations of the little city's anxious economy. It would close
down and get boarded up when the houses in town would get
foreclosed on, and when they'd get renovated and sold, when
they started to become valuable in the eyes of the banks and
the families moving in from up north, someone would come
in and scrub the stone, dust off the vinyl seats, and retune the
organ. The screen stayed small, and the speakers were never
crisp, but it would open its doors and play old movies and sell
tickets for half the price of the other theaters.

The ceiling of the place had been painted navy blue and
purple like a cloudy night sky, and they had inserted tiny little
lights somehow to make it look starry, and if you didn't think
about it, it really did feel like you were watching a movie
outside. We met out front of the theater in our customary silence, delivered nods to one another. He looked the same, but
smaller, older, same eagle's nose and gray hair. We were there
on a weekend afternoon to see some old movie that time forgot. I didn't know whether it was gonna try to make me cry
or laugh. We sat there in the theater, and I stank like tobacco
and grass clippings and exhaust, my fingers stained yellow
and my shoes stained green. It wanted us to laugh, and we
did. We laughed at the goofy actors, the movie a distorted
fun-house version of real life, small and defiant in the corner
of the screen of reality; we laughed for two hours in the dark

under the artificial night sky in between the pillars and the organ, until our faces and our ribs ached — under the laughter, the gentle sentimentality that undergirds the world and keeps everything intact.

I could tell he didn't believe that I was sober, that I didn't drink at all, that he just thought I put the drugs behind me and was starting to grow up, and even though I sensed this, I didn't correct him. I thought there was something true about it, growing at least, something outside of my control. And even though I felt like I was working hard to stay sober, that I was choosing to struggle against instinct, perhaps something had just worn out inside of me, the little glance of friction finally eroding and stopping the perpetual motion machine, that my instinct was evolving or reverting to something baser or finer, that there was no actual fight, just the light contradictions of a heart fluctuating over time.

On the way out, my dad said that he used to go to this theater with his mother, that he remembers seeing *Gone with the Wind* there with her, that she loved American movies, and she used to say they were more real than real life. As we walked to our cars, he looked out across the street at the building there and said, "That used to be a department store."

He pointed over to what was now a restaurant, bar, condo complex. "Above it was a doctor's office where they used to take me when I was a kid."

I saw him gone in his memories.

"I didn't talk until I was five," he said. "They thought I was slow. That was the speech doctor."

I scraped my cigarette against my shoe and looked for a trash can; he was staring at the building, and I said, "You still don't talk."

"Anything you can say, you can say without words," he said.

When I tossed my cigarette into the street, he was still looking at the building, and he said, "The sign is still there." He was right; there was faded lettering running along the corner of the building that said MAAS BROS.

We pressed our cheeks together and he said, "Te quiero mucho," and he got in the car.

My mom opened a drawer by the TV one day and pulled out some notebooks. They were full of detailed, anatomical pencil drawings of animals, plants, and sunsets like those of a naturalist from the nineteenth century. Multiple notebooks, each page with sketches. There would be five pages in a row of the same animal, getting better each time, the lines getting more realistic, swifter, and I recognized the marks immediately as my dad's.

"He's been doing this for as long as I've known him," she said.

I saw him for the first time, like I saw myself, as someone stunted by circumstance, as someone who worked until his body hurt, for decades, but really just wanted to draw little animals as accurately as he could, as someone, just like anyone else, stuck in a world where no one could see the animals of his brain. I tried to look at them the way my therapist from years before had looked at my finger paintings, to deduce some hidden meanings and insights into the psyche of the man who stalked the back of my brain like a silent panther, who was never at the front of my mind, but always approaching me obliquely, surprisingly, conjured up by déjà vus and chance emotions. But the drawings were so accurate, so one to one, that they spoke no secret language, they relied on no lurking ineffable motives. They were drawn in the direct, unmediated language of things, labels in the museum of meaning; when I looked at them, I divined only singular words: *ibis, tarpon, raccoon*.

14

AFTER CLASS, I WENT to the halfway house and shut the curtains and got a couple hours of sleep. I woke up at two in the morning and made some coffee in the common area and went to work. I drove out to the warehouse by the airport where the newspapers got trucked in on pallets, stacked and wrapped up with a strip of plastic. I waited in line with my cart, and I got a couple bundles of papers, took them to my table, and started bagging them. The girl that had the table across from me was real slow, and we always talked while we were bagging. She seemed like a junkie to me. Late September, hot as hell, and she would wear long sleeves. She was pretty, and she always looked like she had the flu.

"I don't know how you bag those so fast," she said.

She was right; I was pretty quick. The bags hung on the side of the table, and I would set up all my bundles on the table so that the cart was empty, and I would grab a bundle, turn it over, rip the plastic tab, fold one of the papers in half, then roll it, and slide it into the bag. Then I'd toss the bag, open end facing me into the cart.

"After you fold the paper, you gotta roll it," I said. "That way it slides into the bag easier." She would just fold them in half and then try to wiggle them into the bag. "And it's better if you turn the stack over, that way you can see the front of the paper through the bag."

"I just woke up," she said. "I always wake up right before I get here, and I'm so tired, it feels like I'm still dreaming. Like, before, I was dreaming about wrapping Christmas presents, putting them in boxes and writing cards for them. And there were cinnamon rolls in the oven, but I didn't even recognize the house I was in. It was like another life. I was wearing someone else's pajamas."

"That sounds like an all right dream," I said.

"And now here I am, wrapping newspapers, putting them in the bags, and it feels like I'm still in the dream."

I was done with my papers, but I figured I should wait for her.

"There was something stressful about the presents. They were late or something, I was in a rush. And I suck at wrapping presents. They were sloppy, and it was actually kind of a nightmare."

I jumped up and sat on my table, looking at her more intently. She was so high, gone off blues, rambling in the opiate stream, feeling that whisper-spine tingle and the gentle itch on her skin. I let my mind run for a second. I had some money now. I cashed all my checks at Amscot and kept the bills hidden in a lockbox under my bed at the halfway house. She took off her sweatshirt, and I could see her track marks, and my heart started beating fast the way it does.

She said, "Where does it end?"

"What?" I asked.

"The routine. Wake up, go to work, go to bed. Sometimes it just feels so stupid."

I nodded. I thought about kissing her and shooting blues. If I stayed away from the uppers, I thought, I could probably keep my mind intact. I imagined us living in a motel room, coming in to run our routes every day, and it didn't seem so bad.

She finished up and we wheeled our carts to our beat-up cars.

"Where's your route again?" she asked.

"I go south, couple neighborhoods down there and some apartment complexes," I said.

She nodded slowly.

"I got these awful nursing homes though. I gotta go in and deliver the papers door to door on the apartments. It's a pain. And the places smell like old people," I said.

We packed the papers into our cars, piled them up as much as we could in grabbing distance from the driver's seats, and said bye. I sat at the wheel for a minute, in a daydream, and when I reached for the shifter, I realized I had forgotten to put my keys in the ignition. I lit a cigarette and tried to just focus on my route. I had started timing myself. I had a yellow stopwatch that I would start as soon as I got into the car. I was shaving minutes off my time each night. I liked this competitive element, trying to beat my personal best. It felt like I was mastering something. Like I was in charge of the night.

As I did the nursing home, I was still thinking about oxys, about watching my blood bloom in the chamber of the needle and slamming it back down into myself. About that heart-soaring feeling and the lightness of it all. So I started to force myself to think about school, and my hands, ink-stained black from the rolling and the folding, were working independently of my head, ripping holes in the plastic and hanging the papers on the doorknobs. At first, I had to carry a sheet of paper with me to tell me which apartments got papers and which didn't, but I had been doing it for a few months now and I'd memorized the sheet a while ago. I needed three duffel bags full of papers to do the first complex, and I had one slung on each shoulder and the other in my right hand, I'd grab the papers with my left, pop a hole with my thumb, and hang it. I didn't need to use my brain for it anymore, and so I had taken to studying while I ran my route.

I put a paper on 208, 211, 214. A little farther, 233, 238, 245.

Not studying from a book, but just thinking over all the material from the classes, quizzing myself, mostly about bio or chem, but Faulkner kept jumping in, interrupting me — *when the shadow of the sash appeared on the curtains it was between seven and eight o'clock and then I was in time again.* I had a test on respiration coming up, and I was going over the chains in my head. I was thinking about the diagrams — glycolysis, the citric acid cycle, the electron transport chain, imagining all the energy moving around according to the strict figures: the circle, the pathways, the enzymes, and the channels. They taught the cell like a factory, like the newspaper warehouse, the folding tables, the route. This was useful for memorization, but I couldn't really believe everything actually looked like that up close. It was too neat. The citric acid cycle, it can't just be a tiny circle of movement inside the cell, that doesn't seem realistic. It was some afterward thing, mapped onto the absolute strangeness and wonder.

301, 309, 310, 318, 322, farther, 341, 347, 348, 349, 350.

It was making it hard to study, the circle and the chain and the diagrams made it seem like a class for kids, like it was so oversimplified that it was worthless, just little colored pictures, purple and yellow and red, to test my memorization skills. When I left the building, I still had one newspaper left in my bag, which meant I had missed a door, but I didn't go back in. Energy goes in, energy goes through a channel, energy gets altered, energy gets used — newspaper comes in, David folds it, David bags it, David throws it, some guy reads it, some guy trashes it. And by the time I got into my car, I gave it up completely, and I was just thinking about Faulkner. I was reciting the passage in my head and under my breath, but I was getting louder in the car. The radio was off.

1240 San Jose St., 1252, 1261, right turn, left turn, 1313 San Ferdinand, 1321.

I had both windows down in the warm night, I was rolling down the street twenty mph, holding newspapers with both hands, tossing out the right window, out the left. I bump the steering wheel with my knee if I need to. My throws had gotten perfect, every paper chopping sideways through the air, spinning like a flat planet, and skidding right to the doorstep. It was a practice, every day the paper weighed something different. Lightest on Monday, then Tuesday, Wednesday has inserts, Thursday has coupons, Friday is light again, and Sundays are the heaviest. Each day needs a different throw. This was my favorite part:

1550 San Obispo, 1552, 1553, 1554, 1556, 1558, 1559, 1561. Right, right, left, right, right, right, left, left.

There was something so satisfying about nailing that section. When the route manager first showed me my route, he did this neighborhood first because it was a little out of the way, but I always saved it for last so I could finish on the San Obispo pattern, a right-left symphony finale. Hitting it felt like hitting the very end of a good book, when the words disappear on the last page, and you stop pedaling and just coast off into the white, into the air, into beautiful catharsis, finally alone, finally released from the burden of gravity and all of those laws and boundaries. *I give it to you not that you may remember time, but that you might forget it now and then for a moment and not spend all your breath trying to conquer it. Because no battle is ever won he said. They are not even fought.*

I still had my one paper left, the one I had forgotten to deliver at the nursing home. And on my way home, I drove over to Bruce's house. I parked my car and walked up to his porch with the paper, looked at the swing where I used to sit waiting for McKay, my shack in the back, black and alone, shifting slightly in the wind. I ripped a hole in the plastic, opened the screen door and hung the paper on his doorknob. Whenever I had an extra, I would do this, just to let him

know I was still working, still showing up, still OK. I hadn't
seen him around in a while. At first, when we were both going
to meetings, we would hang out afterward sometimes, shoot
the shit and smoke cigarettes. I hoped his schedule had just
changed, but I could see a light on in a back room, and I knew
he would never be up this early. And I thought about him in
there, smoking meth, sitting at his computer, howling at the
ghosts closing in at the corners of his sight. And it felt, for a
moment, like he and I were sharing some corner of our souls,
like whatever he was doing to his body, he was also doing to
mine. The meth was traveling through his lungs and into my
consciousness, and I could feel my heart race, the blood over-
flow my ears. I wanted to kick the door in, to gather him up
in my arms the way he had done to me and carry him to a bed
and let him rest and get him food. To buy him an ice cream
cone and just let him know that I was there. But another part
of me, it wanted to go in and sit next to him. To take the stem
in my own hand and disappear back into the chemical smoke.
To disappear from work and class and the halfway house. To
never go back and to run myself down to bone again, like I
had done so many times before.

I looked at the doorknob, and the paper hanging there. I
held my breath, and I asked the world for guidance, I asked
into the dawn. And I let my breath go, and I found something,
a hidden reserve of will that was foreign, like a gift I forgot to
open, and I thought that leaving the paper would be enough.
He would see it whenever he left, and he would remember.
I decided that the next day, I would bring up that I'm sober
around the girl at work. Just mention it, and even it if it made

me feel uncomfortable, she would at least know. It could maybe plant the seed if she ever decided she wanted to try to stop.

Fifty-three minutes, and it was 5:05. I went to my car and I drove out to the sunrise, to the beach, into the warm dawn with the windows down, feeling the empty air against my face.

I ate a sandwich on the hood of my car, and I changed into my bathing suit, enacting the same routine I did every morning. I waded out, and I floated on my back and watched the light fill the air, the sunrise from behind the condos, the tails of fish rippling the water, their little jumps. Birds whistling in the morning. And the sun, which I revolve around, which pulls me in and holds me and spins me, it rose up, and I floated with my ears under the water, the sounds of the Earth muffled or dead, just the low humming of underwater in my ears. I imagine that the land is gone, and the planet is just how it used to be, one hot sea, and I am, like everything else, pre-evolved, a single-celled organism in a fertile culture, waiting for my million-year march up the evolutionary ladder, bobbing and doing nothing, surviving, waiting to crawl out and grow legs and arms and a fat brain.

Watching the sunrise, I thought it might be the end of the world, like the sun was crashing into us and sending everything to hell. The papers I'd deliver tomorrow would say just as much on the headlines. All the water in the sea would evaporate and the plants and trees would wither and die, dehydrated, endless desert top to bottom, side to side. I'd die, and so would everything else, and our physical forms would dry out to dust and blow away in the wind, my dust and everyone else's mixed up and dancing in the wind, until the sun would finally set our dust ablaze, and the fire would raze the whole planet down and down into a little ball of char, and then, poof, like old and spent firewood it would dust up, too, and blow away in some interstellar wind and go God knows where and mix with God knows what, and I'd not be a single thing and neither would anything else.

But it passed, the apocalyptic feeling, and the sun just went regular. And so did I. It stayed far enough away to keep the water like water, to keep the Earth like Earth, spinning two ways like a carnival ride filled with enchanted life, the pull not so hard as to grind me up and not so loose as to let me fly away, sharing time and space with other people being pulled with the same perfect tension. And as this becomes revealed to me, I see the rest of it revealed as well, time laid out like a map. I can point here or there and I can clump up little bits and separate them from the others, compartmentalize them, or I can spread it out in a trail, and I can watch it flow forward like water from a tap. The sun revealed to me the address and schedule of my heart — here now, later there.

On my back with the water in my ears, wearing the Gulf like giant earmuffs, I let the running record of my life slowly fill the newfound quietness in my head. The day, my most recent actions, the most visible ones, results of plot chains extending deep into my subconscious, into sense memories, which, deeper and more inexplicable, more potent than other memories, steep my mind like bones in broth, before being removed and forgotten, but their taste lingers in my consciousness, fills the depth of the day as if they'd never left, as if I were sucking on the bone directly. What are these bones? What strange animal did they come from?

The ice in the cooler is melted, the drinks mostly drunk, mostly empty cans of beer and soda. I could be five, I could be nine. I don't remember. My mom is in a low beach chair, and I am next to her. My brothers and my dad are standing at the water's edge where the waves sometimes are and sometimes aren't. I stand up and walk into the water, so that if I start to cry, no one — not even myself — will notice. It will all just be salty water on my face.

We are there, staring out over the Gulf, watching the sunset. Everything is still, the air isn't moving, and the waves, one inch tall, are gently gliding across the sand like a careful hand over wet clay. It is a cloudless sunset, one whose colors do not reverberate across the sky but instead stay contained to the low parts, the harsh line where the sea meets the sky, but as the light evens out, so does the line, and the sunset, not the typical orange pandemonium but a dim, pink light only a few inches off the sea, is so subtle that you could easily miss it. So subtle that it doesn't even make me sad as I say goodbye under my breath. As it drops, it looks like the dark blue above is pushing the bright color down, rather than it being drawn down by the sinking sun like a shade.

I can hear my dad saying to my brother the same thing he always says on days like this, "These are the perfect conditions for a green flash. Without clouds, the light will bend but not break. It won't be scattered."

I go into the water, and I dunk my head. And as I watch the sun go from circle to semicircle to arc, I can tell it is going to go green. I look back at my parents, at my siblings, and I can see that they see it, too. It drips down, and part of the sun gets shaved off into a little green fleck at the top of the orb. After the sun is gone, only the green dust remains, popping for a moment before it's gone.

What it is, the refraction of light. When the sun is low, its light passes through more of the Earth's atmosphere, and the light gets bent and all of the colors contained within are separated. When there are no clouds and all of the other unseen conditions are in harmony, a person can see it, but supposedly it happens at every sunset. The cool colors — blue, green, and violet — are refracted more than the warm ones because they have shorter wavelengths. All of this, my dad excitedly tells us after we see it, as he has told us before, before and after times that we didn't see it. But now that I am finally seeing it, the explanation doesn't mean much to me. It is the flash itself that I think about. It could be tiny aliens captaining the sun's descent, it could be the color of the sun getting swallowed by the ocean, it could be anything, and I wouldn't care. What is important is that strange hue of green, that light, light emerald which I had never seen before, that shines and glimmers and defies my eyes and then disappears into the sea. Waiting for something I had never seen, trusting that it was real, waiting with discipline and diligence, and being rewarded, that was what I see refracted to me in the green, a drop of strange and beautiful confirmation. That my standing there matters, that it is important, that someone who waits and watches can be rewarded with colors and magic.

After it comes, our little family unit becomes like the cult of the Green Flash. We chatter about it, and as the night gets darker, the trance gets heavier, and we silently play in the black surf and each individually thinks about it, the sunset. Even my mother, who almost never goes into the water, who usually sat on her folding chair and read, and when I or my brother would run up to show her a crab or a shell would put her book down and look at the treasure with genuine interest, even she is in the dark shallow water playing in the moonlight. And as the air and the sea get darker, our splashes start to illuminate more green, bluish green. Running your hand under the water reveals a trail of green dust under the surface. The waves, as they break, send sparkling lines of glitter across the water. It is bioluminescence, my dad says, tiny plankton that store light from the day and shoot it out when they get stimulated by motion as a way of scaring off predators. But once again, the reason doesn't matter. Throwing water into the air looks like lobbing a handful of diamonds into the night. My brother has glitter in his long and curly hair, and when he splashes me, for a second, my body glitters too, little sparks like all of the potential electricity in my body is becoming kinetic. And farther out, the Gulf, like the map of one electric brain, the waves of the second break pulsing and bright in the sleepy water, synaptic activity flashing with all the subtle movements of water and animal.

I see the silhouette of a pelican floating in the moonlight, and I wade toward it. When I get as close as I can, I push my palm along the surface and throw shining water on it. As it shoves off and flaps away, for a split second, as it takes to the sky, its body is full of sparks and it shoots electricity off the tips of its wings before it disappears into the hot night. He flies out over the soft and radiant white sand where the coquinas tumble in with the waves and burrow lazily with the ebb, into the shore where the sand fleas tunnel blindly and thoughtlessly, over the sea oats quivering in the night wind, the thick tangle of sea grape trees and banyans farther inland, out over the parking lots where families pack into their cars, collapsing umbrellas and herding children, loading coolers and chairs and rinsing off their feet, slamming trunks and doors, adjusting mirrors, waiting in traffic to leave, sitting on vinyl seats in sandy, wet spandex. He flies over the bridges where the families speed home, amber headlights extending over purple roads, bodies burnt and happy, heavy from the sun's tender beating, out over the boats humming gasoline and cutting green triangular wakes in the black water; boats still, with engines drawn up, drifting in the current, and their passengers casting lines or weighted nets; more boats gently docked, slapping the tide with each light swell of a wave, straining and tugging their mooring lines, causing them to creak like bullfrogs in a swamp. Out over condos and complexes, their facades populated by a mosaic of windows colored with different shades of light — soft yellow, bright white, television blue, and, some, the old snowbirds', with black glass, dark and asleep — lone lights in the deep night of beach land and coastal forest, and the raccoons and the trash cans, the king snakes asleep in the trees, the pelican flies over all of this and looks up into the night sky, higher into it, into the ends of the hot subtropical air where the atmosphere gets thin and cold, into the stars, the Milky Way, that electric scar jagging across the night sky, the stars falling one by one from nowhere into a deeper nowhere, and above all that frigid space — bird heaven, where the God of Pelicans presides over him and makes sure he eats his fish and floats as he is supposed to, and he looks down into the Intracoastal channel and swoops low away from all that cold black absence and the higher heaven above, and he lands on a pylon, a remnant of a dock whose boards collapsed into the shallow water years ago and is now just a collection of stumps stuck deep into the sand, poking a few feet out of the water. He roosts on an unoccupied post and, with the others, shakes his feathers, drying off, tucking his beak behind his wing, and he closes his blue eyes, and I shoot my imagination back to the water, to the salty warmth on my body, and the plankton and their glitter, and my family. I splash my brother with some water, and we laugh, and I put some in my mouth and spit it out straight up into the air in a line like a twinkling fountain.

I think about what my father said, all the reasons behind the magic, all the molecular little happenstances of the green flash and the glitter, only they don't seem so cold and sterile. They are, themselves, beautiful too, and it is as if all the tiny unseen creatures of the ocean saw the green flash that night along with us, and they stored the memory and the light deep inside their bodies, and this was their fleeting way of re-creating it, that temporary light, of trying to express it and offer it back to the sun. Of course, the color isn't exactly right, but it is color, and it is more than you would expect from those little dancing creatures that are as old as the Earth and the sea. It is more than enough, just to see them try to re-iterate the strange, transient beauty of that particular sunset through their ancient and instinctual planktonic art, to see the water alive with rhythms beyond the scope of my under-standing.